FLIP THE SCRIPT
Why does it always have to be about HIM?

FLIP THE SCRIPT
Why does it always have to be about HIM?

FLIP THE SCRIPT

Why does it always have to be about HIM?

It's not about being the best women to your man—it's about being the best person to yourself. Once this happens everything else will take care of itself!!!

Author: Carolyn Y. Hall

For additional information contact: Carolyn Y. Hall
P.O. Box 134, Dallas, GA 30132.
Email: hallpublishinggroup@yahoo.com

Cover Designed by: Dub-G
Editors: Marvin Williams
       Carolyn Y. Hall

ISBN 978-0-9857948-0-4

Printed in the United States of America

Dedication:

This book is dedicated to all the important people in my life that's always supported me and had my back. Please know, trust, and believe that I love and appreciate each and every one of you in your own special way.

Contents

A LITTLE QUOTE TO LIVE BY:

"In life the things that control you mentally will also control you physically and emotionally."

FLIP THE SCRIPT
Why does it always have to be about HIM?

I'm sure every woman can remember "That" day. You know the day when you fell in love with the man of your dreams. And you couldn't wait to call your best friend, just so you could tell her every single detail. When nothing or no one else in the world seemed to matter, except contemplating the very next time you'll see that person again. Just to share another kiss, another hug, or one more moment of intimacy. Wouldn't it be wonderful if somehow and someway you had a time capsule, and anytime you wanted to return to those good old days you could. Just think about it. Wow, wouldn't that be great?

Knock, knock! Wake up, and let the real world come inside. This is the place where reality hit, and shit happens. Trust me, when love is in the air and things are good, they're real good. And when they're bad, most times they're real bad.

All of a sudden the phone calls come a lot less frequently. Then the kisses move from the lips to the cheek. Hell, sometimes the kisses don't even come at all. And don't get me started on the sex thing. The sex goes from everyday to every other week. And as the sex keeps decreasing, all you notice is the arguments, and disagreements begin increasing.

Honestly, when intimacy in your relationship reaches an all-time low, it sort of reminds me of a drought. When all you need is a little wetness and fertilizer to help your lawn grow, and look its absolute best. But for some strange reason, the much needed rain, never ever seems to fall. Then out of nowhere comes this one sunny day—and you're so fed up, that you dash to your garage, grab a shovel, go outside, and begin to dig. Even if it takes you all day; you dig way deep down into the soil to make sure that you remove all the old grass— just so you can turn right around, and plant new healthy grass.

Let's just say ladies, when your relationship reaches this point, you're the gardener, and your man acting up, should be the unhealthy grass in your yard. And as difficult as it may be—you need to dig way deep down into your soul and remove anything and anyone that isn't healthy for you, and contributing to you looking, and feeling your absolute best. Unfortunately, in this thing called life, the hands on the clock don't stop, and wait for anyone. Instead the hands keep turning, and there's no time to keep dress rehearsing. Eventually, you must make a decision to put all things, and people that have an impact on your life in their correct places and perspective.

If someone loves you, is good for you, and wants the best for you, then whenever they're around; you should feel more *Happiness* than *Pain*—more *Love* than *Hurt*, and more *Peace* than *War*. If these things aren't happening and they're not contributing to your happiness and overall growth as a person—that means they're taking away from it. And that's never acceptable. Always remember, *it's never ok to just settle!*

A LITTLE QUOTE TO LIVE BY:

"It was never him, it has always been you! Take full control of the POWER in your life, and never relinquish it to anyone!"

Chapter
1
Saturday Morning

Here I go again! Another Saturday morning, and I'm standing here staring out my bedroom window, smoking cigarette after cigarette. Words can't even express how frustrated I feel right now! It's no surprise that I'm a nervous wreck, and I can't seem to kick the habit! David always does something to piss me off! If there's anyone that can get under my skin, it's him.

First it started out as an occasional thing. Now it seems like it's every pay week that he pulls the same old stunt. After he leaves for work on Friday morning he doesn't bring his ass home until Saturday or Sunday. Basically, he's gotten to the point where he comes home whenever he gets good and damn ready to. The trip thing about it all is, whenever he does finally decide to stroll in, he doesn't think I should say one damn word to him. As long as I don't ask him any questions, he's all good. He thinks I should be ok with everything he does, and just go with the flow. If I don't say anything, then he won't say anything. He'll act as if nothing's ever happened. He'll just mosey on in the house, and be on chill mode for the rest of the day. But let me question him, it's a wrap. Then he wants to play the blame game, like I'm the one that's causing all the problems. I'm getting so tired of the way he's been treating me lately. I feel as if he's beginning to take me for granted now.

Believe me, if you name it, more than likely I've tried it. I've tried the ignoring him tactic, and not speaking to him once he does finally decide to come home. That doesn't work. It doesn't resolve anything at all. As a matter of fact, that's exactly what he wants me to do. This way he stays out all night, chill with his sorry ass worthless friends, and does whatever the hell he wants to do. And the best part about it for him is; he doesn't have to deal with any consequences from me. He's all good with this approach.

Most of the time, I just go on about my business, and try to forget that he's not at home; but eventually, it gets the best of me. My mind won't let me rest. It keeps wondering, and focusing on him until I finally pick up the phone, and give him a call. Sometimes he has the nerve to not even answer my call at all. He straight up ignores it, and lets it go straight to his voicemail. If I were a betting woman, I would bet that he was right there watching my number come through on his phone.

However, in those instances when he does decide to answer the phone, he always has the same tired ass lie. And I can always tell when he's lying— because he's so bad at it. He starts off by saying, "Baby, you know that I'm sorry, right? You know I go straight to sleep when I start that drinking and stuff." He would go on to say, "So, when I left the club and came ova here to Darren's house, I just fell right to sleep. And by the time I woke up it was way to late for me to drive home, especially with me drinking and all. Plus, you know how picky the police are late at night. It ain't nothing for them to lock a brotha up for the weekend. I'll be home shortly, I promise."

I don't know where he learned how to tell time. But his idea of shortly is hours, or sometimes even days later. To him, that's a good enough reason to stay out all night. But to me, I think it's a bunch of bull! I mean, how many times are you going to end up drunk, and fall asleep on the sofa at Darren's house? Please! And he thinks I'm so dumb that I fall for it, every time. When truthfully, all I'm doing is trying to keep the peace. Honestly, I think the reason he keeps staying out is because he has no real consequences, other than me being pissed off for a few hours, and that's it. But he doesn't care about that. He knows that I'm only going to be mad at him for a short period of time. I'll fuss for a little bit, and then I'll get over it, and that's pretty much the extent of it. So truthfully, he has no real reason to change.

Now David's friend Darren, I can't stand his trifling ass. Darren always has a different woman with him every time you see him, and that's at least three to four times a week. His sorry ass doesn't even have a real job! If you ask him what he does for a living, he'll just lie and say, "I'm an independent business man." He's independent alright. He's an independent full time hustler, jerk and liar. I don't see what all those women see in him anyway. If it was me, I wouldn't give him the time of day! Talk about a scrub. Look that word up in the dictionary, and I promise that you'll see Darren's picture under the definition with a big ass cheesy smile on his face. Because that's exactly what he is, a bonafide scrub. He's just trifling and I can't stand his ass.

But anyway, if you name it, I'm sure I've tried it. I've truly tried it all with David, and that *thinking like the opposite sex* tactic is strictly for the birds. It's hard enough being a woman. I don't have time to think, and be like anyone else. However, when he brings his ass home this Saturday, we're going to sit down, and talk about a few things. He's used up all my patience with this *not coming home every week after he gets paid* stuff. It's just not working for me anymore.

We need to talk about the problems we're having in our relationship. Hopefully, we can try to fix things, and move past some of our issues before things get worse. To be quite honest, things can't get much worse at this point. As a matter of fact, the more I think about it, I'm going to try, and give him another call on his cell phone. I hope this time he'll answer his phone.

Stephanie picks up the phone to call David!

"Well, hello David, thanks for deciding to answer my phone call. I've only been trying to contact you all night. Where the hell are you? I've been worried to death."

"Stephanie, why do you do this all the time? I'm so sick and tired of this shit! Just in case you've forgotten, I'm a grown ass man! As a matter of fact, the last time I checked I'm not married to you or anyone else! And I don't need nobody questioning me every time I'm not at home. I'll be home when I get there. And just in case you've forgotten, my mama's name isn't Stephanie it's Mary, and I don't have to answer to you or anyone else as a matter of fact! So stop checking up, and bothering me. Just leave me the hell alone, and get yourself some business, please! Because if you had just a little then you wouldn't be so focused on me, and what I'm doing each and every second of the day."

"Better yet, I think you need to find yourself a job! If you had a job then you'll have something else to do with yourself all day. And you wouldn't have to spend so much of your free time focused on me all-the-damn-time! I didn't want to go there with you Stephanie, but you took me there. You just get on my last nerves with this dumb shit! Bye, and don't call my cell phone anymore today! I'll be home when I get there!"

David hangs up the phone on Stephanie.

He thinks he's slick. I know him like the back of my hand. He's trying to find something else he can focus on when he gets home. This way he can avoid discussing why he stayed out all night long. I can't believe he screamed at me, and hung up the phone. I didn't have a chance to get one word in. But it's all good. *I'll deal with him when he gets his ass home.* All I did was asked him a simple question, where he was at, and he took it from zero to one hundred in a matter of seconds. This is dead give-away, and I know he's guilty of something. His attitude is so nasty towards me lately. I really don't know who he is anymore. He's not the same person that I've known, and loved all these years. Something or someone's making him change. I don't know what it is. But I'm gonna find out real soon.

I wonder if it could be that our age difference is finally getting to him now. I know that I'm seven years older than him, but it's never seemed to matter to him before. As a matter of fact when we first met, this was the very thing that he loved about me. He would often say, "I love a mature woman." *Lately, I've been hearing on the news that some men have been going through this mid-life crises thing a little earlier than others.* Maybe that's it. At least, I hope that's it. This would help to explain some of the *outbursts,* and *bizarre behaviors* he's been displaying lately.

Regardless of what's going on between us, I know he loves *our* children. Ever since we've been together, he's always treated my daughter Monique, just like she was his very own, and I've treated his son Devonte the same way too. Even though we both had children from previous relationships, we've never shown any favoritism among the children. We both try really hard to make sure that doesn't happen. *This is a difficult situation for anyone to be in. He really has me puzzled, and I just can't figure out what he's thinking.*

I'm so hurt right now. I love this man with all my heart. As far as I'm concerned, he's my soul mate. I may be blind, but I'm not stupid. I understand what love feels like, and I haven't felt it in a very long time. However, what I have felt is total disrespect, neglect, heartbreak, and pain, and it doesn't feel good. Just to make things even worse, I have this stupid tattoo on my lower back that reads: "David's property." Hind sight is always 20/20, and I don't know what the hell I was thinking when I did this crazy shit! I just feel trapped right now. Sometimes it seems as if I'm in a scary movie, and there's no way out. I'm damned if I do, and damned if I don't. But regardless of what's going on between the two of us—I'm sure when he gets home we'll get things worked out. I can promise you that much. We have to if our relationship has any chance of surviving. The biggest issues we have in our relationship are communication, compromise, and trust. I'll just have to wait and see how everything goes once he comes home. However, the longer it takes to for him to get home, the more anger I begin to feel. I hope I can keep a cool head once we begin to talk. If I don't things are going to get real ugly, real fast. And that's not going to do any one of us any good.

A LITTLE QUOTE TO LIVE BY:

"A strong sense of self is not called being selfish it's called handling your business."

Chapter
2
The Argument

As I lay here restless in my bed, all I can say is wow! It's now Sunday morning at 8:37A.M., and David still hasn't made it home yet. Every time I hear a car pull up, people talking, or a telephone ring I think it's him. But it never is. Finally about twenty-two minutes later I hear the front door open and it's him. He has some nerve. I can't believe David hasn't been home since Friday morning when he left for work. Of course he'll use the argument we had on Saturday as the reason he stayed out even longer. He's full of excuses.

I can hear David walk into the kitchen, and open the refrigerator. He begins to make himself a sandwich. Even though I can't see him, and he hasn't said a word I know exactly what he's doing. Everytime he comes home from his weekend binges he's always hungry. I can even hear him placing things on the counter in the kitchen. He's so predictable; nothing in his routine ever changes. He walks into the family room, and turns on the television. Unknowingly to him, all this time I've been laying hear in bed listening to his each and every move.

An hour later he finally decides to come into the bedroom. Of course he's still giving me the silent treatment. He doesn't even make eye contact with me. Then he goes directly into the bathroom to take a shower, still not saying one word to me.

If my memory serves me correctly I can't remember David ever taking a shower this long before. He thinks he's slick, but I know exactly what he's up to. He's trying to avoid dealing with me on any level. I'll give it to him this time. He's won the W*aiting* game.

Since he's taking forever to finish showering I think I'll get up and make myself some coffee. My first thoughts were to pack up, and leave home for a couple of days. Maybe this would teach him a lesson. You know, change the game up a little bit, so I can give him a taste of his own medicine. He would never expect for me to do anything like that, because I never challenge him on anything that he does. However, the way I'm feeling right now is he shouldn't dish it out if he can't take it. But then I began to think about things a little more. What *the hell was that going to accomplish? I'm going to leave home upset, and when he doesn't call to check up on me, I'll just return home even more upset. If I did something like that, and it backfired, I would look like a new fool when I returned home.* So I decided to stay home, and face his ass! We*'re going to handle this situation the right way. Like two grown adults. I mean, we are still in love, or at least I am.*

When David came out of the bathroom I was sitting on the edge of the bed waiting on him, coffee in hand and my cigarette in the other! I'm sure he could see the smoke coming out the top of my head because I was furious with him at this point. I turned my head in his direction and cut my eyes at him, in an effort to express my deeply rooted frustration with him. I finally decided to break the silence, and I asked him *"What's going on with you?* What have I done so badly that you have to disrespect me the way that you do? You don't come home for days, and when you do finally come home it's so late you may as well stay out for the rest of the night! You don't hug me anymore! You don't say you love me anymore! You tell me I'm fat every chance you get, or you simply imply that I'm fat! You don't give me money like you use to. You barely give me enough money to pay the bills. What's going on with you? Is it that I'm not sexy enough for you anymore? Answer me! Tell me what's wrong with you! Is it anything I can do to help make things better? David, you know how much I love you! I want things to be like they use to be between you and me!"

Are you going to respond?

David ignores Stephanie, and continues to go on about his business.

"Look at you! It's like everything I just said to you went in one ear, and straight out the other. I can't believe you're ignoring me like this. You keep getting dressed, rubbing lotion on your legs, and arms, checking your text messages, and whatever else you feel like you want to do just to avoid answering me. What's that all about?"

Finally, David turns and says, "Stephanie please stop nagging me. I don't think you can handle the truth! Ok, I really don't! So let's just drop it, and leave well enough alone alright! I don't want to talk about anything that has to do with us right now! It's not the right time. And Stephanie, you know the old saying, don't keep looking for something, because you just might find it!"

"Yes, I do know the old saying, but I can handle whatever you have to tell me! I just want the truth!"

"Alright Stephanie, the truth is…I love you. But I'm not in love with you any longer! A lot has changed since we first met. When I first met you we couldn't get enough of one another. I loved everything about you! You loved everything about me! No one else could even come close to you. You were my all in all. However, over the last couple years you've changed."

"You don't care about how you look anymore! You've gained so much weight! And it aggravates the hell out of me that you keep blaming your weight gain on having these kids. You know it's not the truth because you've gained even more weight after the kids were born. And most of all you question me to damn much, and I don't like that Stephanie! In fact, I hate it! I hate the way you question me like I'm your child or something. I don't like it at all! The last time I checked I'm a grown ass man! To be honest with you—I feel like we've grown apart in our relationship. Our needs and wants are not the same anymore. That's all there is to it. Now are you happy?"

"I gave you what you've been asking for didn't I? I put everything on the line, and gave you the raw truth. This is how I'm feeling right now at this point in my life. And frankly, I don't see things getting any better, any time soon between us. So where do we go from here? The ball's in your court now."

"Yes, I'll give you that much. You gave me exactly what I asked you for. You told me how you feel. And I'll have to take that. But to be honest with you I'm kinda shocked. I didn't realize the state our relationship had gotten to this point. Based on everything you just said it seems as if you can barely stand the sight of me right now. And for some strange reason, you seem to place all the blame on me for everything that's gone wrong in our relationship, and I don't understand how you can do that. Everything's not my fault! You're not perfect either."

"Stephanie, that's not completely true. I never said that I was perfect, not by any means. I know I have some things I need to work on but..."

"But what? Trust me David, you may not have said it directly, but you definitely implied it more than once. But it's ok, and since we're being completely honest with each other. It's only right that I let you know how I've been feeling lately. For the last several months things have gotten worse. You walk around the house most times, and you barely say five words to me. You pretty much ignore me all day. Not one week goes by that you fail to remind me that I'm unemployed, and I don't contribute financially to our household. How do you think that makes me feel? I know you think there's no real value in being a stay-at-home mother, and partner. However, if you had to pay me a salary for all the things I do; quite frankly, your ass couldn't even afford me. I'm sure you can care less about all this right now. But it takes a hell of a lot to run a household and make sure that everything flows the way it should. Believe me, it's not an easy job. I just make it look that way."

"Whenever there's a problem with the kids at school—I handle it! I don't even bother you with those issues. I try to make sure you have as little stress in your life as possible. You curse at me anytime you get good, and ready. It's as if I'm not significant to you at all anymore—like I'm not a real person, someone without feelings. You don't even have the smallest amount of respect for me. Never mind me, but you're not even setting a good example for our children treating me the way that you do."

"Stephanie, what the hell are you talking about? I think we better end this conversation right now before things really get out of control! I don't like it when you bring the kids into our disagreements; especially, when it has nothing at all to do with them."

"What do you mean this has nothing to do with our kids. It has everything to do with them. Whatever directly affects me; indirectly affects them. I think you fully understand what I'm talking about. Of course it would be better for you if I just ignored all those facts, wouldn't it? But I can't! So please remember any decision you make, doesn't only affect me. It affects our children to."

"Stephanie, you're to much!"

"To much! What do you mean, I'm to much! Tell me how is our son supposed to learn how to treat his girlfriend or wife in the future, if he only has you to look up to? Tell me how David? The time has come for you to step up, and own that. Our son deserves to have a positive role model in his life—someone he can call for advice when he needs it. But not just any man. He deserves to have a positive influence. Someone that can teach him how to earn his way in a world that can pick you up, and spit you out! For the longest period of time I thought that person was you. As a matter of fact, I knew that person was you. If you can't change for me, you should be able to change for our son, because he needs you more than ever right now."

"What are you talking about? I've never let our kids see me doing anything inappropriate. And I've always been a good provider for our family. And regardless of how our relationship ends up the kids will be ok. I'm sure of that! So please don't try and use the kids to hold onto what we once had—because it's not going to work."

"So you don't think our kids notice when you're mean to me? Even though they've never said one word I'm sure they notice when things aren't going well between us regardless of how hard we try and hide it."

"Of course they notice. I expect them to. They're not little kids anymore, and they're very smart. I'm sure not very much will get pass either one of them."

"I agree. That's why I'm so concerned, David. During those times when you weren't treating me the way that you should; I constantly forced myself into believing that you didn't realize what you were doing. When the truth was, deep down on the inside of my stomach, I knew I was covering up my true feelings, and lying to myself."

"In case you haven't noticed, over the past several years, you've really taken my self-esteem down to its lowest point, and believe me I know you don't care! You really don't give a damn! I guess that's very unfortunate for me because I still care. I wish it wasn't so difficult for me to detach myself mentally from you! But it's been one of the hardest things I've ever had to do in my life. I've tried and cried, and cried, and tried—but when you have a heart and love someone it's just not that damn easy to let go. At least for me it's not!"

"Stephanie, I never said I didn't care about you. And I can only speak for myself; but I know that I need a change in my life right now. I just wanna be honest with you. Hopefully, one day, you will understand this."

"David, the point isn't whether or not I understand. It's just that nothing about this situation is easy for me. Put yourself in my shoes for one moment. Would you be happy if your life was being turned upside down right in front of your face, and there was absolutely nothing you could do to stop it—regardless of how much you wanted to?"

"Of course not Stephanie, I never expected for you to be happy with all this new information. I'm not that insensitive, and out of touch with your feelings. And whether you want to believe me or not—I do understand why you're feeling the way you are right now."

"David, I appreciate all that. However, I really don't think you have a clue how I'm feeling right now. My heart is so heavy, and I've been trying with all my strength, to wake up from this nightmare of a conversation we've been having—but I can't wake up from it! I just want you to be honest with me. Are you seeing another woman? Have you been screwing someone else? Because lately, I know you haven't been making love to me! Regardless of what you believe I'm not as stupid or naive as you may think I am. I just keep a lot of hurt bottled up inside. I'm nothing like you. I always think about your feelings, and put you first before I say, or make any moves. I don't just say whatever I'm thinking."

"That's always been one of my biggest problems, and I never could shake it. But since we're being honest with each other, I feel there's more to this story than what you're telling me? You talk about me gaining weight, so what I've gained weight! You've gained weight over these past seventeen years to. Your hair is thin—your belly is big. And it seems like you've gone from being

Big Daddy to Fat Daddy. And don't get me started on your attitude, because it's just awful. You try to control me with the money, because you know I don't work and you feel I'm at your mercy. And I don't like that at all! But do you hear me complaining about every single thing? Well do you? No you don't! I just put my best foot forward and try to make the best out of a bad situation. That's all!"

"I know you do Stephanie."

"To be honest with you David, if anyone should be upset, it should be me. We've been together for over seventeen years, and we were never married. Now you want to up and leave me high and dry with nothing to show for all these years we've been together, with the exception of our two children. Don't misunderstand me. I love our children. However, outside of them I really have nothing else to show for all the years we've been together. Absolutely nothing! Whenever I would ask you about getting married—you would avoid that question like I was asking you for your first-born child or something. I never understood what that was all about?"

"To be honest with you, I never understood where all these changes were coming from all of a sudden. David, I really don't even know who you are anymore! You're not the same person I met years ago either. Any mature adult should know with age comes change;

especially, when a couple has been together for as long as we've been together. You should know there's going to be some type of change. Some changes will be for the good, and some for the bad. But that's life, and we're not exempt. But for some strange reason, you seem to only recognize the changes in me. When the fact is, we've both changed. However, the biggest difference between you and me is I still love you, and I'm willing to accept the changes in you. But you're not willing to accept the changes in me and I think that's pretty sad."

"David, is there something you want to say?"

"No Stephanie, there isn't!"

"What do you mean? No, there isn't! Ok, so what's next for us? It's obvious we both have things we need to work on. I'm willing to work on them, if you are."

"Hello David, do you hear me?"

"Yes, Stephanie, I hear you! How can I not hear you? I just don't know what else to tell you!

"What!" You just don't know what else to tell me! What you should be telling me is you're not leaving your family! That we're going to work on our problems! That's what you should be saying."

"Instead you're standing there, staring at me, looking stupid!"

"I would really like to hear something positive from you for a change. I feel that I deserve that much."

"Stephanie, I can't tell you that right now! I can't tell you what you want to hear! I can only tell you the truth based on how I'm feeling. I have to be true to my own feelings for a change."

"Oh really, so you're telling me, it's easier for you to walk away from everything that we've shared over these past seventeen years, than it is for us to work on things? I can't believe that! I thought our relationship meant a little more to you than that! Our family should mean more to you than that! Is our relationship that bad, it's not worth a second chance? Is that what you're telling me? Are you really done with us? More importantly, are you done with our family? Look at me David! Put your arms around me. Touch me, kiss me, do something please! I want to feel your touch again. Show me that you care just a little bit!"

"This isn't the right time Stephanie."

"Why isn't it? Making up has always been sweeter for us. I feel like I'm begging you to love, and be with me, and I don't understand why! We have so many years invested in each other, and we've shared so much, how can you just throw it all away like this? You just can't!"

"Say something! You had a lot to say a few minutes ago when you were saying all those ugly things to me. Now you're acting like the cat's got your tongue. Will you say something to me? Answer me! Please!"

"Alright, you don't turn me on sexually anymore! You don't satisfy me! I want a woman that's not so sexually reserved—someone that's more of a free spirit, and willing to try new things sometimes. That's how you were when we first met; but now you've changed. You act so old fashioned! Whenever I ask you for sex, you always say you don't want it this way, and you don't want it that way. I'm just tired of it all! You never want to try anything new! And the only time I see lingerie, is in the magazines. You never wear sexy lingerie to bed! All you ever wear are those ugly, hot ass cotton pajamas with the flowers on them! It looks like something my grandma use to wear. And when it comes to oral sex, please, you don't want any part of that anymore—when we use to do it all the time! You've gotten so boring, and in the box! You said keep it real with you, right? Well, that's what I am doing. This is as real as it gets."

"Sometimes, when I get home from work, I want to be surprised. I want my lady to answer the door for me, butt-ass naked. The only thing I want to see on her is titties and ass. And if I am driving, I might want my lady to satisfy me right there on the spot. Sometimes a little rub down might hold me until I get home, and I don't feel there's anything wrong with that. I want my lady to keep things right and keep things tight. If I say baby, I wanna make love to you right now, I want her to ask me, '*baby how you want it?*' I don't want her to ever tell me *No*, or put me off until the morning. You always give me this same old shit about you being tired. And the trip thing is, your ass don't even work! Oh yeah, and if I'm feeling a little freaky, I might want a little anal sex. You've made it perfectly clear that *Hell* would freeze over before you do that! Man, you would've thought I'd asked you for your right leg or something. You would always say something like this, 'Boy, please, you done lost your mind! You know I don't get down like that! I've told you over and over again to stop watching all those Porno flix, because you know I'm not down with all that freaky stuff! You ain't going to mess me up for life. When it comes to back there—the only action is coming out, ain't nothing going in, and I've told you that before. So please stop asking me, because I'm not changing my mind!'"

"You don't even try to spice things up when it comes to our sex life. That's why I don't ask you for sex anymore like I use to—because it's always the same old thing, the same old way, all the time and that's so boring to me."

"Oh really David! So it's like that now? Who is she? Is she White, Black, Latino, or what? Just be honest with me. I'm a big girl! That's what you call me sometimes anyway, right? Trust me I can handle whatever you have to say to me!"

"Stephanie, you can't be serious! This is exactly what I'm talkin about! You ask me to tell you how I feel, and when I do, you get all mad, and act like a crazy woman! Then I have to deal with a whole new set of problems that I don't have time for. This is why I just keep my mouth closed, and handle things the way that I do. I don't have time to deal with all the extra headaches, and nonsense from you!"

"Really David, if the truth be told everything you just said sounds like an excuse to me. For some reason, you think you're the only person that's been dissatisfied with our sex life lately. But that's absolutely not the case. To be honest with you, your sex game hasn't been on point here lately either. I don't know who she is, but someone has you thinking the tip of your penis is made out of platinum or something, wrong answer! To be quite honest with you, my kitty hasn't purred in a very long time for you either. As a matter of fact, it hasn't even meowed. So please don't think you've been handling your business ova here, because you haven't been. Trust me! And let me just touch on bed room attire for a quick moment. Those briefs you wear to bed every night ain't getting it done over here either. To be honest with you I absolutely hate-em! I'm sure you know the ones that I'm talking about—the stained raggedy white ones that sag in the back, and are ripped on the waist. Yeah those, I guess in your mind, you think those are real sexy to me, huh? Please, don't get me started on that subject! Trust me it won't be a pretty picture."

"Stephanie, see this is what I'm..."

"Oh yeah, please answer this one question for me. What makes you think I don't enjoy making love? Has it ever occurred to you that making love is more mental than physical for me? Whether you know it or not—*there's a direct link between how a woman feels emotionally, and how she performs sexually.* If a woman is feeling loved, and she's happy in her relationship—to be honest with you, *she can climax without any penetration at all.* All it takes is the *right person, with the right touch, in the right place, at the right time, and she'll keep coming back for more.* To the contrary, if she's *unhappy in her relationship, the way she responds sexually will be very cold, and despondent. She'll just go through the motions, and fake it all, and you'll never know the difference!*"

"Don't get me wrong, on those days when things are hectic and time is of the essence, it's ok to skip over the appetizer, and go straight for the entrée. In those cases, yes, sex will just have to do. Get it in when you can."

"As for me, whether you know it or not, I prefer having it all. I want the entire meal, and I don't like skipping anything if I can help it. I want to be romanced, kissed in all my special little places and sweet nothings whispered directly into my ear. I like it the old fashioned way. When a man really knew how to treat a woman, and made her feel special. These are the little details you seem to skip all over when you make love to me, and it shows. That's why I respond the way that I do when it comes to sex. I have wants and needs too whether you want to believe it or not. Everything's not just about you, even though in your little world you're the only person that seems to really matter!"

"Whenever we do have sex which is very rare, all you want to do is jump right into things. There's no intimacy at all. You don't kiss, touch, or rub me in the right places like you use to. It seems as if the only thing you want to do is hit it, and leave—like I'm a booty call or something. Some random chick you just met in the club the night before—you will never ever have deal with or to see anymore. And I don't like that feeling! As a matter of fact, if all I wanted was a quickie, I can handle that all by myself. And I'll be completely satisfied when it's all said and done. Trust me; I don't need a man for that! I don't need you for that! I want a man to make love to me and connect to me emotionally—not just have sex with me physically!"

"You can care less if I ever have an orgasm or anything else as a matter of fact. The only person you seem to care about is yourself, what makes you feel good, your pleasure, and getting your release and to hell with me or how I'm feeling, and that's not fair to me. But regardless of all this I try to remain positive, and keep things moving on the strength that eventually we'd rekindle the spark we once shared. However, the only vibe that I keep getting from you is resistance. I may be wrong. But in my heart I feel it's because our relationship no longer consist of just the two of us. I think you're seeing someone else."

"Don't just stand there, and look at me with that stupid-ass look on your face! Who is she? I know there's someone else! Who the hell is she! David, don't leave this bedroom! That's what you always do! You always walk out on our conversation, and we can never get anything settled."

"David!"

"Answer me damn it! I know it's another woman! That's the only thing that can explain the way you've been acting lately. Why is she such a damn secret! Do you plan on walking away from your family? I want to know now! You owe me that much, at the very least!"

"No, I'm not walking away from our kids. But to answer your question, yes, I'm leaving our relationship! I'm trying to make arrangements to move out now! And if you must know, I have plans to move in with my boy Darren, not some other women."

"Excuse me, what did you just say?"

"I said that I'm making plans to move out now!"

"No not that!"

"Oh Yeah, I'm moving in with my boy Darren. I'm going to give you a little more time to get things together. I don't want to leave you high and dry without anything, especially with you being unemployed, and having our kids and all.   I'm not that insensitive regardless of what you may think right now. We have shared our lives together for the past seventeen years; please give me a little credit! So how much time do you think you'll need to get things in order?"

Stephanie turns toward David. and gives him a little smirk.

"What did you just say?"

"You know, how much time will you need to get on your feet? I have plans to take the kids to Orlando in two weeks. And I will explain everything to them at that time."

"Our kids are old enough to understand that sometimes people grow apart. Sometimes relationships change. And I think that's what's happened to us. We've just grown apart, that's all! Don't worry, I'll handle everything with our children. You don't have to worry about that. Let's face it. They're not little kids anymore. Jaylen is sixteen, and Mya is fifteen. They're both in high school now, and make good grades. And just like we've said before— we know the children can feel the tension between us. And that's not a good thing."

"Well, well, isn't this some shit to say! What the hell do you mean? This is what's happened to us! That we've grown apart! No, that's not what's happened to us! That's what's happened to you! I've always loved you! My love for you never ever waivered! I feel the same way about you today that I felt when we first met seventeen years ago! So David, please don't speak for me. Man-up and speak for yourself! Don't make me your escape goat, and pull my feelings in with yours because that's not how I feel at all."

"I thought we were soul mates. Boy was I wrong! I was dead-ass wrong! But you know the old saying; *don't assume anything because you make an ass out of you, and me.* I guess you can say the joke was on me, right?"

"Why would you say that Stephanie? This isn't a joking matter at all!"

"I never said it was! This is far from a joking matter to me. This is my life! So I need for you to listen to me for a quick minute. Let me ask you a few questions because it's obvious there are some important events that have slipped your memory. Tell me who do you think was there day and night when you had that horrible motorcycle accident and you couldn't even feed yourself? It was me! Who the hell was there when you couldn't even wash your *stankin* ass? It was me! Who loved you when everyone else turned their backs on you, and said you were a worthless piece of shit? Again, and again, it was me! It was me then, and it's still me now! And again, just like you've done in the past the only thing I seem to get in return is your behind to kiss!"

"Despite everyone's advice I still stayed with you! It wasn't because I had to! I stayed with you because I love you! You were hurt, and I wanted to be there for you! Most importantly, I stayed because I didn't want to lose you! And I still don't want to lose you! I need for you to help me understand what I can do to help fix our relationship? If it's my weight, then I will lose weight. I can get my hair done more often, if you want me to. I promise to stop arguing so much, and I won't question you as often if that makes you happy. I just want us to try, and work on our relationship! But I need your help, because a relationship consists of two people. I can't work on it alone. I will do whatever it takes because I still love you. I can't explain it—but I feel having you in my life is much better than you being gone."

"Stephanie, believe me it's not you! It's me! I need some time to work on myself. That's it! I don't want to hurt you anymore, but I can't be in this relationship any longer. And if I stay I know I will continue to make you unhappy, and I love you to much for that. I didn't want to upset you, but I have to be honest. How can I make you happy if I'm not happy within myself?"

"I don't want to compromise my happiness anymore! I've done this long enough! And to be perfectly honest with you, I just want to be free! I feel at this point in our lives ending this relationship would be the best thing for the both of us. And it's better if we end things now, while we're still friends."

"We have to face it. Our relationship has run its course. It's time for the both of us to get off this ride. At least we can still be friends. I can't speak for you but for me, our friendship means more to me than a broken relationship. I feel that our destinations are not the same anymore. We're on different paths now. I love you, but I'm not in love with you. I'm so sorry Stephanie, but I have to get on with the rest of my life! And I suggest you do the same."

"You may not agree with me now, but one day you'll realize this decision was the best thing for the both of us. Don't get me wrong. I'll always appreciate everything you've ever done for me. You were my right hand for many years. There's no question about your loyalty. You had my back, and I will always be grateful to you for that"

"But Stephanie, I can't repay you with my life, for the rest of my life! Just think about it. Would that be fair to either one of us, if I stayed with you out of obligation? I don't think that's what you want. Just like you said before with life comes change, and at this point in my life, I'm ready for a change. I don't feel I can do us anymore!"

"Wow, you really just said a lot. So this how you truly feel?"

"Yes Stephanie, it is. Even though it's hard for me to leave—it's even harder for me to stay. I'm sorry, but this relationship is over. I hope you can understand—because, if the shoe was on the other foot I would understand. I'm sure you would agree holding on to our good memories, means much more than us staying together and making bad ones. We have to think about the kids. We can't continue to be selfish, and only think about ourselves. A one-parent household that's full of love is much better than a two-parent household that's dysfunctional. Can we at least agree on that much?"

"David, you've given me a lot to think about. However, it doesn't change the fact that I'm still in love with you. All I can do is hope and pray every day that it's not to late before you wake up and realize you let a good woman go."

"Yeah, I know."

"I hear what you're saying. And I can sense the attitude in your voice. However, I don't think you fully understand the impact of the decision you're making. But it seems like I have no other choice but to accept it."

"There are no other options for us anymore, Stephanie. The time has come for us to move on with the rest of our lives."

"Ok, well I guess your mind is made up then!"

"Yes, it is! I want you to understand this decision is what's best for the both of us right now."

"It's whatever David!"

A LITTLE QUOTE TO LIVE BY:

"True love doesn't hurt. It should be the calm after the storm, the peace after the commotion, and the rainbow after the rain. When your relationship begins to feel and look like those old shoes in your closet, you know the ones that have holes in them, but they still fit well and feel real good, that's when you know it's time to throw them away. Never compromise your happiness, and peace of mind just to be with someone else."

Chapter
3
Bank Accounts

Hello Daja...

"Hey girl, what's going on?"

There's complete silence on the phone. The only sound is Stephanie sniffling.

"Hello Stephanie, Stephanie, what's wrong with you? Are you ok? Stop crying! You're scaring me! Why are you so upset?"

Stephanie again sniffles. Then she responds.

"I'm sorry Daja. Yes girl I'm ok. I know I should've waited to call you when I wasn't so upset. But I really needed someone to talk to. Do you think you could stop by the house a little later on today? David, and I had this really big argument yesterday, and I've been crying non- stop. You wouldn't believe how nasty he was to me. I can't believe after everything we've been through all these years, he had the nerve to tell me that he didn't want to be with me anymore. Can you believe he's already in the process of making plans to move out and leave me, and the kids?"

"What? You've got to be kidding me! He's a poor excuse for a man! As a matter of fact he doesn't deserve the title of a man! He's a slithering snake, and I can't stand his ass. I expected for him to pull a move just like this eventually. I knew it was just a matter of time. If I were a man, I would've kicked his ass a long time ago. I'm sorry Stephanie, but he just gets on my last nerve, and I mean my very last one."

Daja, I know you can't stand him, and your anger's coming from a good place. But I need you to focus on me right now. Do you think you'll be able to stop by later today, because I really need to speak with you?"

"You know I'll be there as soon as I get off from work. Unfortunately, this is my weekend to cover the phones. I can come by after 5:00P.M. today, if that's ok, unless you need me to come now."

"No Daja, please don't leave work for me. I'll be here when you get off later today. Also, when you have a break please give Cindy a call for me and ask her if she could stop by around 5:00P.M., also. Tell her to come only if she has some free time. I know she may have to pick up the kids from daycare. But at least ask her for me, because I don't want her to think that I left her out."

"Sure Stephanie, that's not a problem at all. I'll call her as soon as I can."

"Are you sure, you're ok?"

"Yes, I'm sure. Trust me. I'm fine, or at least I think I'll be."

"Alright Stephanie, I'll see you later on today."

"Ok."

David's walking around the house with an attitude. He still hasn't said one word to Stephanie since the argument.

"So David, where are you going?"

David just keeps walking and doesn't acknowledge Stephanie's question.

"I know you hear me!"

"Out, Stephanie! I'm heading out, if that's ok with you!"

David grabs his keys and leaves out the door as Stephanie watches him drive off.

"Just look at him. I know he can see me standing here at the door. I guess he doesn't feel he owes me an explanation anymore. Especially, since he's put me on notice that he's moving out and moving on."

"Actually, I was glad David left because about 40 minutes later Daja and Cindy drove up to check on me. Now we can talk freely, since he's not hanging around trying to listen in on our conversation.

Stephanie hears a knock at the door and it's Daja and Cindy.

"Hi ladies, come on in. Thanks for stopping by to check on me."

"Girl please, you know that's not ever a problem."

"So, how are you doing?"

"Truthfully, I've had better days. But I'll make it."

"So have ya'll had a chance to talk anymore?"

"No, Cindy, he really hasn't said two words to me since the argument."

"He really has some damn nerves."

"Yeah, I know Daja. All he's been doing is walking around here with a chip on his shoulders, like I've done something wrong to him."

"Stephanie, I know it's hard for you to do right now, but time will heal all your wounds. You just have to focus on yourself and the kids right now. Ya'll are the ones that really matter, not him!"

"You're right Daja. But girl, it's not that easy when you've been with the same man for so many years. You know that I've never cheated on him, right? I've always believed in being a faithful woman. And now it's come back to bite me."

"Yeah, I remember when we had that conversation. All I can say is it couldn't have been me. I've always made it perfectly clear how I feel about

David. I never felt he deserved your loyalty. As long as I've known you, he's never earned it. Trust me. I don't have a problem with a woman being faithful, as long as her man appreciates her being that way—and he reciprocates the treatment. But he never has. If it had been me, I would've had me a real man on the side a long time ago. He wouldn't have had the time to leave me. His ass would've been out the front door, like the trash he is. But what goes around comes around, and he'll get his. You can stick a penny in that one, and wait on your change! That's one person that will get what's coming to him. I just hope I'm around to celebrate when he does!"

"I thought that he would appreciate me being faithful. But obviously he didn't care. And the worst thing about it all is I've been crying all day, and night and he hasn't cried one time. Isn't that something? He has no compassion for my feelings at all."

"Trust me this has been a long time coming. I know it's hard for you to see right now but everything will work out for the best in the end. You'll see."

"Thanks Cindy."

"Don't worry, Stephanie. We've got your back, girl. Don't worry about a thing. You can count on us day or night—but you have to promise to call us, and let us know what's going on, because we can't read your mind ok."

"Ok. I promise."

"Well enough about him for the day. It's time to talk about the real business at hand. So Stephanie, what are your plans? Have you handled your business yet?"

"What do you mean by that?"

"Did you and David have any joint bank accounts together, any stock," bonds, cds, or other property?"

"As a matter of fact we do. We have a joint checking, and savings account. The stock is in his name only. It was issued through his job. The cds are in both him, and the children's name. My name isn't on the cds."

"If I were you, the bank would be my first stop tomorrow morning! I would withdraw every dime out of those accounts. You know that you're not working right now. And you're going to need that money to help pay the bills, and take care of these kids until you get a job. You can't depend on him to do anything for you. I just hope he hasn't been to the bank already. "

"I doubt it. Normally, he doesn't handle that type of stuff. He probably hasn't even thought about it to be honest. I would be totally surprised if he's taken any money out of either account already. However, lately he's been full of surprises. So I just can't be to sure. The last time I checked, we had $5319.00 in the checking account, and $755.00 in the savings account."

"Wow! That's good, girl!"

"Yeah, I know. We've always done pretty well when it comes to saving money. That was one of the best things about our relationship. I'm really going to miss that about us."

"Ok Stephanie, stay focus."

"Alright Daja, you're so crazy girl."

"I really wish you had called us sooner. But that's neither here nor there right now. At this point, all you can do is go to the bank tomorrow and check things out for yourself. We all just have to pray for the best."

"You're right. That's all I can do now. I feel so much better since you ladies stopped by today. I really wasn't thinking to clearly."

"Girl please, this is how we do it. When one of us feels weak, we have a responsibility to pick that person up. That's what friends are for."

"Well I'll call you'll in the morning to give you an update once I leave the bank."

Ok.

Daja and Cindy leave to head home and Stephanie showers and go to bed.

It's Tuesday morning and Stephanie arrives at the bank and is speaking with the bank teller.

"Good morning, how are you today?"

"I'm doing great. How may I help you?"

"Yes, I need to make a withdrawal from my checking and savings account please."

"Ok, do you have checks or a debit card for those accounts?"

"Yes, I have a debit card for both accounts."

"Ok, please slide your card through the machine. Then enter your personal identification number, and I'll be happy to take care of this for you."

"Thank you."

"You're welcome."

There's a pause while the teller reviews her account.

"So ma'am, how much did you say you were trying to withdraw today?

"I would like to withdraw $5300.00 from my checking and $750.00 from my savings please."

"I'm sorry ma'am but we have a slight problem. It appears that someone has already made a large withdrawal from this checking account yesterday and there's only $2.00 available for withdrawal."

"What! You must be mistaken! Are you sure that you've accessed the correct account?"

"Yes, I'm sure. I'm looking at your checking account information on my screen now. Would you like for me to check your balance in your savings account?"

"Yes, please!"

"Please side your debit card for that account. Then enter your personal identification number for that account and I'll provide you with your balance information."

"Ok, thank you."

"I hate to give you this information ma'am. But the same thing has happen on this account also. Your savings account only has $4.21 available in it for withdrawal."

"What in the hell's going on! How could he do this to me? He's taken everything! I mean everything! He barely left $6.00 between both of the accounts combined. I can't believe this!"

"Thank you so much ma'am. I truly appreciate all your help. I know exactly what's happened to all the money in the accounts."

"I'm sorry I couldn't be more help to you"

"It's ok. Thanks again."

Stephanie leaves the bank upset and almost in tears. She can't wait to call Daja and Cindy to let them know what's happened.

"Hello Daja…"

"Hey."

"He did it! He went to the bank yesterday and withdrew all the money out of both bank accounts. Can you believe that shit? I can't believe that I let this happen.

I'm always a day late and a half a penny short. I'm so mad right now. I can just scream! You have no idea!"

Stephanie is talking and crying hysterically!

"Calm down Stephanie. Please don't drive until you calm down!"

"I won't. I'm still parked. I just didn't expect all this, not at all! And now all the money's gone too. I'm so pissed right now!"

"I know you are. But there's nothing you can do about that money. It's gone now. You just have to charge it to the game. That's all."

"Tell me something Daja. Why do you think all this is happening to me? Am I that bad of a person? I feel if it wasn't for bad luck right now, I wouldn't have any luck at all."

"Stephanie, you know I'm not even going to answer that question, right. Bad things happen to good people all the time. It's not that you're a bad person at all. The real problem was you were to good, to long, to someone that didn't deserve you. That was the problem! I'm not going to sit back and allow you to attack your character. I'm sure David will do enough of that for the both of you."

"You're right."

"Stephanie, I don't want to seem insensitive to what's going on in your life right now. Because trust me, you know that I'm not. I just don't want you to begin blaming yourself for any of this. None of this is your fault! It's all his. Just ask him about the withdrawal when he settles down for the night. Tell him you went to purchase some food today from the grocery store and your card was declined. You couldn't understand why, and when you went to the bank, you were advised that there was no money in the account. Then sit back and let him put his foot in his mouth."

"That sounds like a really good approach. One of my biggest concerns is rather or not he'll pay the rent this month. I'm really worried about that. Hopefully, he won't be that low down, and not pay it. He surely has to realize that his kids will need a place to stay, and I won't be the only one he's affecting if he doesn't pay it. I'll just have to wait, and see how things go once we talk tonight."

Stephanie decides to wait about five more minutes before she drives off.

Wow, I've truly had a long day today. I'm going to lie down and rest a couple hours before he gets home.

Stephanie's been sleeping for about six hours when David walked through the door. She is awakened by the door closing behind him—but she decides to wait a little while before going into the living room to speak with him.

"Hello David, I need to speak with you for a moment."

"Ok."

"Do you plan on paying the rent this month? It's due in two days."

"Yes, I do plan on paying the rent. Why are you asking me that question?"

"Don't play stupid with me. I'm sure you know why I'm asking you that question."

"No, I really don't!"

"I went to the grocery store today to purchase some items for the house and my debit card was declined. When I went to the bank to find out what the problem was—I was advised that there was no money in either one of the accounts. That's why I'm concerned."

"Alright, I understand. And you're right! I did withdraw all the money out of the accounts yesterday. Have you forgotten that you haven't worked in years? So if you think about it, all that money in the accounts was really mine."

"What! No one could have every told me you would end up being such a jerk, not in a million years! You just made the statement that I don't have a job, and the money is all yours, right? So tell me, how the hell are all these bills supposed to get paid Mr. Working Man? You could have at least left me something! You weren't even considerate enough to do that much! You took pretty much every dime!"

"Do what everybody else does. Get a job! And I didn't take everything. I did leave a few dollars in the bank so the accounts would remain open. I didn't have to do that much!"

"Please don't tell me you're talking about the $2.00 you left in the checking account and the $4.21 you left in the savings account?"

"Yes, that's exactly what I'm talking about! I could've let the bank close both of them. But I didn't!"

"Well, as far as I'm concerned you should have! What the hell am I going to do with $6.21! Give me a damn break! You know what, I'm done with this conversation! If I keep talking to you, one of us will end up spending the night in jail! I can promise you that much!"

"Yeah, I think that's what you better do!"

"And what if I don't? Then what are you going to do?"

David gives Stephanie this disgusted look. He then grabs his keys and leaves back out the front door.

"Exactly, you'll do what you've always done— leave!"

A LITTLE QUOTE TO LIVE BY:

"A woman that makes her own money makes her own rules! Don't ever depend on someone else for your total financial support!"

Chapter
4
Two Months Later

"Lord, I'm coming to you on bended knees! My grandmother has always told me to talk to you just like I would talk to her; that you don't come when I'm ready, but you always show up on time. Well God, the time is here and the moment is now, and I'm leaning, and trusting on my grandmother's words of wisdom, because I'm in need of your strength, right now."

Sometimes I feel I can keep going. I've lost someone that was a big part of my life for many years, and my spirit is broken. He's taken all the money out of the bank accounts, and I hardly have any money saved to live on. Even if I wanted to move on I truly don't know how to. I'm so broke right now, it's even hard for me to pay attention at times, and nobody seems to understand how I'm feeling. Sometimes I feel there's a stranger lurking somewhere deep within my spirit; because this is a place so dark, and lonely, even I don't recognize it. If it wasn't for the help of social services I wouldn't have any money at all, and my check is only three hundred-fifty dollars a month, that's barely enough money to buy groceries and put gas in the car. Not to mention I haven't been able to make a full rent payment since David left. It's been a huge struggle trying to juggle this lil bit of money, and make ends meet. And to be quite honest with you, most times, the ends just aren't meeting.

David didn't even pay the rent before he left; even though he promised me that he would. I don't know why I continued to believe his sorry, lying ass (oh Lord please forgive me, that slipped). I have payment arrangements on all my utilities. And if I don't make a payment within the next couple of days my lights and water will be turned off. I'm just so tired of being tired. And to top things off, the landlord personally delivered a letter to me advising me if the rent isn't paid by Friday he would have to evict me from the house, and I don't know what I'm going to do. I don't even know where I'm going to stay. I know I could stay with my friends—but I really don't want to burden them any more than I already have.

Lord please believe me; It's not that I'm stupid, or naive; however, even with all this going on in my life, I can't seem to stop wondering what I could have done to make David happier, then maybe he wouldn't have left. If he was still here, I know I wouldn't have all these financial problems to deal with right now. At the very least he would've made sure all these damn bills were paid. On the other hand, I would've had to deal with his constant lying, and that may have been even worse than being late on my bills. It's nothing I hate more, than a liar.

I'll take responsibility for gaining weight. Yes, that was my fault. I didn't have to let myself get to this point. And I regret every night, as I lay here lonely in this big old empty bed, that I rejected him so much. If only I could turn back the hands of time. I would do so many things differently. But I can't! So "Lord, I'm leaning on your word right now. I need your help! I need for you to give me the strength I need to move forward with my life, because I'm not strong enough to do it on my own."

"I know I need to be strong for my children, but I can't even be strong for myself right now. I can call on my friends-but I need a divine intervention that only you can provide. I'm looking to you and not anyone else to help me deal with this situation. I know when prayers go up blessings come down. So I'm standing here in line, and I'm waiting on mine. Please hear my prayers. In Jesus name I pray Amen!"

I'm so glad today is Thursday morning. I feel it's going to be a good day for me. I'm scheduled to see my doctor at 1:00 P.M., and hopefully he can prescribe me an anti-depressant medication because I need to relax my nerves right now! I feel depressed, and jittery most of the time and my actions are so unpredictable. You would've thought I had a bottle of caffeine or something, but I know it's just my nerves. However, I can't seem to shake it for nothing.

Every since David left I haven't been able to eat. I haven't been able to sleep, and when I call David just to speak with him about the children he won't even answer his phone. Even though it's been two months since David has left I'm still struggling to get past the hurt, pain and disappointment that I'm feeling inside. I have more bills than I have money. It's like my life is stuck in neutral right now, and my heart is so heavy. I keep crying all the time. I mean the stupidest things people say seem to make me cry, or think about David and all these bills that I have. My life feels like it's spiraling out of control, and there's nothing I can do to stop it. And to make things even worse my friend Daja called and told me she saw David at a popular night club in downtown Atlanta Saturday night. I guess he didn't waste any time moving on, unlike me.

Of course, I had to ask her a few questions like, *was he alone, or was he with his stupid friend Darren*? I can't even stand to say Darren's name. He was a big problem in our relationship. He always had a different woman around. And he flaunted his bachelor life style in front of David all the time, and I will never forgive him for that.

Well to get straight to the point, let's just say Darren's not a size eight. He's not tall and tanned. And he surely doesn't have long black hair. Oh yeah, did I forget to mention that Darren also doesn't have a big butt or small waist either? So, you do the math. This is one of those times I begin to think to myself, *damn, what I didn't know surely didn't hurt as much as what I do know now.* But I had to open my big mouth and ask questions about David ass anyway. Hine sight is always 20/20. But that's one question I should've just kept to myself.

I really wish Daja would've never even told me she saw him in the club! It hurts me so much to hear the truth when it's about him. I tried to be strong and cover up my emotions while Daja was talking about him, but it didn't work. I'm sure she could hear it in my voice. I was sniffling, and crying like I had lost my damn mind. Boy-oh-boy, I hate loving this man so much. And this *hurt before you heal thing,* ain't worth a damn.

When David finally left, I went through so many emotions. My emotions went from sad, to mad, to down-right angry! I went through all of these emotions in what seemed like five seconds, and I could feel each emotion coming on again, especially, after I heard the update from Daja. My mind again began to wonder and here I go again with the pity-party. I set up all the decorations, and everything. The problem is, no one showed up to the party except for me.

That's when I began to think to myself *David never wanted to take me out.* Whenever, I would ask for him to take me out, he would always give me this lame excuse like, "Baby, it's only going to be me and the boys tonight. All the ladies are staying home. We're just meeting up to play few hands of spades, have a few drinks, and chill for a few hours. That's it. You really wouldn't like the atmosphere. "Trust me Stephanie it's not your thing." This is the bull David would always feed me.

He would then give me a quick kiss on the forehead and head his ass straight out the front door. I can still smell his cologne. He always smelled so nice when he left. I always wondered why he had to smell so nice, just to meet up with his boys. Now everything's coming full circle, and it makes sense to me now. The sad thing is he would always have the same whack-ass story week, after week, after week. The location and activities may have change, but everything else stayed the same. Nevertheless, I was so in love with him that I didn't see the writing on the wall. Now I often question myself, did I not see the writing on the wall? It was definitely there. It's been there for many years. I mean, David was never a good liar. I just chose to ignore it? I think subconsciously I convinced myself to believe that having a morsel of a man was much better than not having a man at all. Little did I know I was sadly mistaken!

As I stare at the ceiling, I begin to think to myself *this is a damn shame. How could I love someone this much, and this hard? How could I love a man that obviously doesn't care about me? He really could care less how much hurt and pain I'm in right now.* I did everything with the exception of getting on my knees to convince David to stay. I wanted to try and save our relationship regardless of the cost, but he still made a decision to walk away. The sad thing is he didn't just walk away from me; he walked away from our children too. The more I thought about it, I began to realize that David was a selfish, self-absorbed little boy. He wasn't a real man and he only cared about what he wanted in life. He didn't give a damn about the life we had as a family for the past seventeen years, so how could I expect for him to give a damn about me.

The more I thought about it I began to realize love shouldn't hurt so much. If he ever really cared about me at all then love should've brought him home every night! Instead, he chose to hang out with his friends, and be by the side of another woman. But that was his choice. At the end of the night he did have a choice. And he chose to go with what was behind door number two. He did what most men do. He thought with the head located between his left and right testicles, and not with the one between his ears, the head that the good Lord gave him. But he'll eventually get his. He'll soon find out the grass is not always greener on the other side of the fence. It just looks that way, when you're on the outside of the fence looking in! And the old saying that *coming to stay ain't like coming to visit,* is a true statement. He'll find out for himself, sooner than he realizes and I can't wait. Trust me, every dog has his day. David's definitely a dog. And his day is certainly coming! Grandma would always say "Don't burn the bridges that brought you cross, because one day, you just might need those same bridges." All I can say to this bridge is burn baby burn. And he better hope I'm not the one he needs to bring his ass some water when he gets thirsty!

A LITTLE QUOTE TO LIVE BY:

"Most times the rainbows in our lives can't fully form, and show all the bright colors they have within. This is because we hold onto clouded memories that should be cleared away. Everyone has a rainbow inside of them, if we just allow the sun to come in and shine."

*Chapter
5
Eviction Day*

I knew the time would come that I would get evicted for not paying the rent. It was early Wednesday morning about 8:45A.M., the kids had just left for school on the bus, and it wasn't more than fifteen minutes later before I heard the doorbell rang. Then I heard a very loud knock at the door. The knock was so loud it scared me. I rushed to the front door to see who it was, and it was the police!

The police was there to evict me. I must say I was caught off guard, a little scared, and most of all embarrassed, but I knew this day was coming at some point, because I was already served an eviction notice. Before I could completely open the door; tears began to roll down the front of my face. The only bright light in this situation was the police showed up in the morning, and most of my neighbors were already gone to work, at least the ones that have a life were already gone. That did save me a little embarrassment, but not very much.

When I answered the door, the only thing I was wearing was my robe. The police told me that I had to leave the house immediately, and that all my contents would be placed on the street. In my weakest voice, I replied, "Yes sir." The policeman was so rude. He didn't care what I had been going through. He was just here to do his job. At the end of the day, that was exactly what he did. I really couldn't believe what I was hearing. Even though I knew this day was coming I wasn't mentally prepared for it. I mean, how can anyone ever get prepared for something like this, especially, if they don't have any money saved to move?

I should've tried to move my things out of the house earlier, but I couldn't afford to put anything in storage. So I just waited and hoped that things would just go away, or magically get better. But nothing got better. In fact, things got worse. After I spoke with the police I immediately ran to my bedroom so I could get dressed. Everything was happening so fast, the only thing I could think to do was call my Uncle Eric. I was so nervous when I called him. My hands were literally shaking as I dialed his number. My uncle was the closest family member that I could call and get a response from right away. I was crying like crazy as I explained to my uncle that the police were at my house and I was in the process of being evicted.

As I was on the phone, I could hear the eviction company moving all my things around and out of the door. It only took about an hour or so for them to get the house totally cleaned out. Pretty much everything was gone!

I mean all my worldly possessions were out on the street. Then the police put a lock on the door to ensure that I would not go back into the house. As I sat on the end of the curve, and waited for my uncle to arrive my mind began to reminisce about my life. I don't think I've ever cried so much in all my life but I began to think to myself, Wow, everything that I've ever owned is right here on this curve. Everything was thrown out on the street like old filthy rags. It was as if the last seventeen years of my life didn't mean a thing to anyone, except me. My hurt was so deep down on the inside of me that I couldn't reach it even if I tried. I was numb to reality. Nothing around me seemed real. It was like I was in a fog or something. I was right next to the highway, but I couldn't hear a sound. It's crazy, and I just can't explain it.

My uncle finally arrived with the rental truck, and I noticed that he brought my cousin James with him. James works for a moving company, so I knew it wouldn't take us to long to get my things loaded on the truck.

It took us about two hours to finish. Once we were done loading my stuff, Uncle Eric said that he would help me pay my storage bill until I found a job. I was so grateful for my uncle. I don't know what I would've done with all my things if he hadn't offered to help me out, because I had no money. I was dead broke and my spirit was even more broken.

With everything going on, I almost forgot to call the kids school. I wanted to make sure that they didn't ride the bus home today. I didn't want the kids to be surprised, and embarrassed when they got off the bus, and notice that all of our stuff was gone. School was out at 3:30P.M., and I wanted to make sure I was there waiting to pick them up. I had to stand outside of the car, because the kids would not expect for me to be in my uncle's car. Once they were in the car, I explained to them what happened today, and that we would be living with Uncle Eric until I found a job, and got back on my feet.

One of the many things I love about my kids is that they are very mature for their age. Both of them were fully aware I had been struggling to pay bills every month since David left. And even though I'm sure they will miss having their own rooms, both of them understood our living arrangements would be temporary. Nevertheless, they were both perfectly fine living with Uncle Eric for a while. As I continued to drive to my uncle's house, everyone in the car was completely silent. Mya was unaware that I was looking at her in the rear view mirror on the drive home, but I did notice a few tears rolling down her face. I asked her if she was she ok, and I reminded her that she could talk to me about anything that was on her mind. She just looked at me and said, "I'm fine mama. These tears aren't for me, they're for you." I just hate to see you going through all this by yourself, that's all. But I know we'll be just fine. I'm sure of it."

I then turned to my son Jaylen, because he was sitting there as quite as a mouse, and I wanted to hear from him also. I asked him how he was doing, and he said, "ma'ma I'm ok." I guess he wanted to be strong, and not shed a tear. But a mother knows when her kids are hurting.

I turned to both of the kids and said to them "I don't want you'll to worry about me, because I'm going to be alright. The best thing the both of you can do for me is make sure you keep your grades up in school. That's what really matters to me most of all. Everything else will work its way out."

I knew the move would be an adjustment for all of us. Uncle Eric did have his own family. However, he didn't even give it a second thought before opening up his home to the kids and me with open arms. I must admit, we were a little cramped. All three of us had to share the same bed. However, at least we had food to eat every night. Plus the alternative would've been much worse. We could have been homeless, with no options at all.

Even though I appreciated everything my uncle was doing for the kids, and me, I'm going to do everything in my power to get through this situation, and get on my feet as quickly as possible. I don't want to be a burden on my uncle and his wife Diane for very long. But I thank God for the both of them, because even though my uncle said yes, his wife could've said no, but she didn't. And I will be forever grateful to the both of them for that. I'm sure most people will agree. This is a terrible situation for anyone to be in, especially when you have children. However, sometimes life's most valuable lessons come out of bad situations. And because of this adversity, I have learned one of the most important lessons of my life.

A LITTLE QUOTE TO LIVE BY:

"You can't appreciate where you're going in life if you don't recognize where you've been. Your past is the building block for the future. Therefore, use it as a guide, and not an excuse."

Chapter
6
The Mirror

It's now Monday morning, and it's been three whole weeks since I was evicted from the house. I'm still waiting to wake up from this nightmare of a life I live in. As I walked towards the bathroom to wash my face, and prepare for the rest of my day I happen to look to the left, and I noticed this lady in the mirror. She has features of someone that I thought I once knew. However, this lady looked as if she carried the world on her shoulders. Her eyes were puffy with dark rings, and hair hadn't been combed in days. She appeared physically, and emotionally drained. She was totally neglecting herself, and worst of all, downright stank. If I didn't know any better, I would've thought this lady had nothing to live for, and no one loved her.

So I walked a little closer to the mirror to see if I could get a better look at this lady. Once I got really close I began to realize that I did recognize this lady. It was me,

Stephanie! But my spirit was so broken, and beaten down I hardly recognized myself. I looked so sad, and I didn't like what I saw in the mirror. I didn't like what I had become.

Seeing the woman in the mirror was a vital turning point in my life. I made up my mind that things were going to change in my life. I had no choice, things had to change!

How can I talk about David being selfish and leaving our kids when I was just as guilty as he was? No, I hadn't walked out on the kids physically, but I had checked out on them mentally and emotionally. I just left them in a different way, that's all. With the exception of conversation the children and I had on the way home from school. I really hadn't taken time out to speak with the kids about their father leaving. For some selfish reason I felt if I didn't talk about him it would hurt a little less, and maybe things would just go away.

Honestly, I wasn't any better than David was if you think about it. In fact, I was worse. I was ma'ma. I'm supposed to be strong; the backbone of the family. I was supposed to be the rock, and I was failing miserably at it!

A child without their mother is a sad child indeed. I realized that even though I may be broken and bruised emotionally. I wasn't dead, and it was time for me to get it together. I continued my steps toward the restroom. I then sat down to use the toilet, and once I was done handling my business, I turned on the shower, grabbed my wash cloth, and soap. Then I made my way into the shower. I turned the water up as hot as I could handle it, and I let the water run down my face, and the rest of my entire body for a very long time. Once I lathered my rag, I began to scrub my entire body. Unknowingly, I began to scrub harder and harder with each scrub. It seemed like I was trying to scrub all my problems away in this shower. I must have showered for over fifty minutes; until the water began to get cold. It was then that I began to cry so hard! I screamed so loud! I didn't realize this was exactly what my soul had needed this entire time. I felt a much needed release. I felt like I was finally free and letting go of all the baggage I've been carrying around for so many years. And it felt great! Believe it or not, I felt great!

This is when I made up in my mind. The same woman that stepped in this shower would not be the same one stepping out of this shower. My plan was to leave the old me in here. And I had planned to leave the pain I've been feeling right along with it! And that's exactly what I did.

If David didn't love me anymore, then that was his loss. As a matter of fact, he didn't deserve me! I finally realized that I had to stop blaming him. It wasn't his fault it all was mine. He couldn't make me do anything I didn't want to do. I made the choice to stay in the relationship for as long as I did. I stayed because I wanted to; because I wanted him. I had to look at myself and place the blame in the right place! David is who he is. He knew right from wrong, hurt and pain, and so did I.

He did exactly what I asked him to do. He kept it real with me. I told him I was a big girl, and I could handle whatever it was he was dishing out. I guess I forgot to mention to him that I didn't like the Bullshit entrée he was serving up!

Nevertheless, after my constant questioning, David gave it to me, just as I'd asked him to. He gave it to me straight, real straight, on the rocks, with no chaser!

A LITTLE QUOTE TO LIVE BY:

"Loving yourself unconditionally is the best love of all, and there's no one qualified to do a better job than you can."

Chapter
7
Self Analysis

I wish I could afford a personal trainer. I know I would feel much better if I lose a few pounds. This weight thing has always been a struggle for me. After the kids were born, let's just say—it's been all downhill from there. I've gained over forty pounds with my last child, and it seems like I can't stop gaining weight, no matter how hard I try. Truthfully, I really haven't tried too hard. But I've thought about it real hard, if that counts for anything. My face is so fat. And every time I'd wave to someone, it was like my arms had a mind of their own. I mean, even after I've stopped waving, the fat under my arms just continues to do whatever the hell it wants to do. And don't get me to talking about these fat ass thighs. Every time I walk, my thighs rub together. They're huge. One time they rubbed together so much, I actually got chafed. And that's not to be funny, because that crap really hurts. Just listen to me. Everything I hate for other people to do and say about me, I do, and say about myself. At times it seems like I'm my own worst enemy. I really need to stop and get a grip.

In retrospect, how can I expect for a man to love me, when the truth is, I don't even love myself. I'm just as bad as the average man. I only focus on my physical. I'm my worst critic.

I sometimes even ask God, Why me? I know that I shouldn't question God, but I don't understand why some women are so beautiful, and seem to have it all. And then there's women like me—the type of women that seems to not have very much at all, not even self esteem.

It's almost like we're empty shells walking around with a lot of insecurities. I guess I can understand it just a little bit, because the physical is the first thing people have to judge you by. I've never heard a man say, "Baby, I really like your personality" when they first meet you. And I really do have a great personality; if they would just try, and get to me know me first. It's really sad to live in a world that's so judgmental. But it is what it is.

I guess every attraction starts with some type of physical aspect initially. To be quite honest, there's only one time to make a first impression. I don't know. I guess people in the world shouldn't be so shallow, because if you only focus on the physical appearance of a person, you might miss out on an opportunity to meet a very nice human being.

My mom loves me so much. She always says, "Stephanie, you're such a pretty girl. Take a little time and fix yourself up a little bit, and put on a little make-up before you leave the house, because you never know when you'll meet your husband."

I'm just the opposite of my mom. Whenever my mom steps out the house, it doesn't matter where she's going, she always put on a little makeup and dresses nice. That's just my mom. What can I say, she's a real Diva! I wish I had just a little of her confidence. If I did, chances are, I'd be much better off.

Honestly, I've always been the type of mother to put my children first. As long as they were taken care of that's all that really mattered to me. I've always thought my family should come first. This is what a mother's supposed to do, or at least that's what I thought. But I think the time has finally come, for me to change my game up a little bit, and that's exactly what I'm going to do.

I'm going to give my girl Daja a call to see if she knows the name of a good personal trainer. I want to get started on a workout program, this way I can lose some weight, and tone up at the same time. Daja never liked

David. She never appreciated the way he treated me, and she called him out a long time ago.

Daja has always wanted me to leave him. This is one of those times I should've listened to her advice. But like a lot of women, I was in love. As far as I was concerned, David could do no wrong in my eyes, when actually he was doing a lot wrong, for a long time.

One thing about Daja is if you're relevant in Atlanta, then you're on her radar. She seems to either know all of the important people, or she knows someone who does. Daja's my Atlanta connection. So, I will ask her to hook me up with one of the finest male personal trainers in the "A." I mean I need to have some eye candy to keep me encouraged when I work out.

Just like I thought, my girl came through. She connected me with this fine, and did I say, fine-ass trainer? She not only connected me with him, Daja got him to train me for free. Well at least until I find a job. I was so happy, because he did not have to do this for me. But since he was good friends with my girl Daja, he did it as a favor to her.

My trainer's name is DaShaun. And when I saw DaShaun for the first time, I thought to myself, *Damn, this man is fine*! I must have just died and gone to heaven. I wanted to drop, and give him fifty right then on the spot! You noticed, I said I wanted to drop and give him fifty, because, if I would've dropped down to attempt just one push up, I may have needed some oxygen just to get up. I'm just sayin '.

When DaShaun and I met at the gym, we introduced ourselves to each other. Then we started to discuss my personal goals. He wanted to know what I wanted to accomplish. Most importantly, he wanted to make sure this was something that I wanted to do for myself, and that I was dedicated to working out and eating right.

I was so happy. This was the first time, in a long time, I had a conversation with a man, and he sincerely wanted me to do something just for me.

Once DaShaun, and I got through the formalities, we both decided that my first training session would begin on Saturday morning at 9:00A.M.

The next day after my first workout session, I was so sore. I could barely move, even my eye lids hurt. I began to think, *what have I gotten myself into?* But my motivation was DaShaun. I couldn't stop thinking about seeing his tall, dark, and handsome, fine-ass. I mean every part of this man's body had muscles. Just thinking about him made me instantly begin to feel better. And after the first couple workout sessions the workouts began to get much easier.

Eventually, I began to feel I had to work out. My body began to crave going to the gym. Working out was now something I didn't have to force myself to do anymore. And the best part about this situation was that I'd already lost fifteen pounds. Not only did I feel good, but I looked even better!

Oh Yes, and I can't forget DaShaun; he's another added bonus to my workout routine! All I can say is DaShaun is um, um, good to the eyes. He's so sexy! Whenever, I see him my hormones just go crazy! I mean, I haven't been this close to a man in such a long time that gave a damn about me, in any way shape or form. If he knows like I know, he better not rub against a sister, because I can't be held responsible for my actions. Please believe, I will plead the fifth if I have to.

He always compliments and encourages me to keep going even when I'm tired and frustrated, and I appreciate him for that. He's young in age but he has an old soul. His ma'ma has definitely taught him well. He's truly learned the art of hugging a woman from the inside out, and I love it! DaShaun, and I have never spoken about each other's relationship, but whomever the lucky woman is in his life, if she knows like I know, she better keep him real close, because men like him are hard to come by. He's very nice, works hard, and most of all he's learned how to make a woman feel real special on the inside.

Oh Yeah, how can I forget—he's fine as hell too!

A LITTLE QUOTE TO LIVE BY:

"The way you feel on the inside, is what shows on the outside. Always remember, the way you felt yesterday isn't the same way you must feel today. Get the most out of each day God has blessed you with, and use it as an opportunity to start fresh, and anew."

Chapter
8
Lunch with Daja

"Hey girl, thanks for the lunch invite. Wow, it's been such a long time since I've been downtown to eat lunch, and it feels so relaxing. So Daja, how's everything been going with you lately?"

"I'm good. You know me. I'm just trying to do me. You know what I mean?"

"Yes, I feel you girl."

"Ok Stephanie, enough of the small talk, you know I need an update. So how are things going with you? And how are the kids adjusting to all the changes that have been going on lately? Because from what I can see, you look like you are doing just fine. You look great! You look like you've lost about twenty or more pounds. Am I right?"

"Well, you're in the ball park. But to be exact, I've lost fifteen pounds, and still counting. And I feel so much better. As for the kids, they're holding their own. Of course both of them miss their dad a whole lot.

"I'm sure they do. What about you? Do you still miss him?"

"Well, when David first left home it was a complete roller coaster. And it wasn't just the kids that felt this way, because I was feeling tripped out also. Sometimes, I still have my days, but overall I'm trying to keep it moving, and get on with my life. But I would be lying if I said things were perfect. I mean, I loved this man with all my heart for many years, and I never even considered stepping out on him, not even once! Maybe if I had stepped out on his pathetic ass then our break up may not have been so hard for me to deal with. You know what I mean?"

"Let me clue you in on the latest stunt David tried to pull on me. All I can say is he really tried me, but I bet he won't pull that card again. Ok, this is the deal. David called me on Thursday night to ask me if he could come, and get the kids for the weekend, because he wanted to spend a little time with them. Of course, I said yes. So, when David got to my uncle's house he knocked on the door to let me know he was outside. As we were talking, I happened to notice there was a girl in the front seat of his car. And why did I have to see that? Girl, that's when things got on-and-poppin'. I went off on his ass! I was like. 'You have some damn nerve bringing that skank over my house to pick up my kids!' You noticed that I did say my kids because his sorry, broke ass ain't worth the dust in his pocket!"

"I asked him, 'What are you thinking.' And while I was speaking to him, this heffa had the nerve to get involved in our conversation. And why did she have to do that? You would've thought the gates of hell, just opened up. I told her, if she didn't shut the hell up, I was gonna come out there, and shut her up. I guess she wanted to pull my trump card, and be Ms. Save-a-whore-for-the-day."

"David tried to calm me down. But the more she kept talking, the angrier I got. You know he wouldn't let me go until I punched his ass in the balls. When he reached down to grab them, I finally managed to get around his ass, and get to the car where she was standing. And before I knew it, I punched her dead in her mouth. Then I grabbed her little ass, and pulled her out of the car. I gave her the ass whippin' her momma should have given her. I bet next time she'll be on her best behavior when she comes to another woman's house. I must admit. I released some old and new shit on her ass. She picked the wrong one to mess with that day. I did feel kinda bad afterwards, because she had to take the whipping for all the otha mess I've been going through lately. I've had a lot of issues to get off my chest and I think I released all of them on her that day! I was praying that no one called the police on us, especially, since I'm staying with my Uncle Eric, and his family. I didn't want to bring that foolishness over to their house. It would've been so embarrassing if the police had shown up. I'm so glad things ended much quieter than it started."

"I'm not sure what got into me. At the time, I just felt he totally disrespected me and so did she. And all I could see was red. Her big mouth didn't help things either. It wasn't enough for him that he had already hurt me to my heart, and sent me to one of the lowest points in my life; he had to bring another woman to my house just to top things off. I felt the least he could do is show me some respect, as the mother of his children. Please believe me, and trust what I say! He'll think twice about pulling that stunt again. And I bet the next time, she'll shut the hell up, when she's told to do so."

"There's nothing worse than another women thinking she holding things down, and being disrespectful; like she's the head-women-in-charge. I told her, 'Girl' you better stay in your lane! Because, this ain't what you want! All I can say is, it's been a real emotional struggle for me, Daja. I just take life one day at a time. At this point, that's all I can really do."

"You know the old saying? 'In life it's not what you go through, but how you go through. All I can say is, I'm really going through.' Other than that; I guess it's all good! It is, what it is."

"Wow, that's crazy. You didn't even call me and tell me you had all this going on."

"I knew we would be meeting up for lunch so I decided to wait to tell you in person." Well enough of my drama. I just want to give you all your props!"

"Props, for what?"

"Where did you find DaShaun? All I can say is: *where has his fine ass been all my life?* And when you talk about eye-candy; Lord have mercy! He's not just one piece of candy, he's the whole jar. I get a toothache every time I see him. It really should be a sin to be that fine, that's all I can say."

"How did you meet him? Have ya'll ever kicked it, or anything like that, because I know that he's hard to pass up? You know a sister needs to know."

"Girl please, no ma'am. He's like a little brother to me. I met him at the gym about two years ago when I was working out one day. I needed a little help using one of the exercise machines, and he was walking around the gym so I asked him if he could show me how to adjust the bar on the exercise machine. He said yes, and once he was done demonstrating how to use the equipment, I let him talk me into signing up for a few personal training sessions. Ever since then, we've been really close friends. But that's as far as our relationship has ever gone. We're strictly platonic friends; that's it!"

"Ok great, that's good to know, because you know that I love myself some tenderloins."

"You're so funny Stephanie. Are you still working out with him?"

"Yes, he's my incentive to go to the gym. My sessions are twice a week. He's still not charging me until I get a job. And I really appreciate him doing that for me. But I'll make it up to him once I start working. But yes, I make my workout sessions faithfully."

"Oh yeah, I almost forgot. I have some more good news to tell you Daja! I have a job interview next week with this company in Fulton County. I applied for an accountant position. I hope I get the job. You know that I really need it. I feel this will be another great step in the right direction for me. I have a hair appointment on Saturday after my workout session, and my interview is on Monday. I've already brought a new interview suit, and some nice shoes to wear. I will keep you posted on how things go."

"That sounds great, Stephanie. I'm so happy for you. I'm going to send up a big prayer for you, because I know God's got your back. I see a big change in you already. Even though I know things may not have been easy for you lately, you are much stronger than you give yourself credit for. You're going to be alright. I have no doubt about that.

Make sure when you go into the interview room that you make eye contact with the interviewer, and be confident. Just claim that job and you'll get it. I promise it will work for you. That's what I always do. Confidence goes a long way, trust me, the way you feel on the inside always show on the outside. Walk confident like you know the job is already yours. And you'll get that job! Always remember, what God has for you, is just for you, and no anybody else. But it's up to you to go out and get it!"

"Thank you Daja. I know I can always count on you to help lift me up when I'm feeling down. Wish me luck and I'll call you on Monday after my interview to give you an update."

"Stephanie, you don't need luck, you have God in your corner, and that's all you need. Trust me!"

A LITTLE QUOTE TO LIVE BY:

"When the ride gets to tough for you to handle, that's when you let go and let God carry you the rest of the way. God never promised us that our lives would be easy. We can only hope that it would be fair!"

*Chapter
9
The Interview*

I made it to my interview about thirty minutes before time. I knew that I looked great, and I felt even better! Mr. Jackson called my name to come into his office so that I could begin the interview process. Once I sat down across from Mr. Jackson, I began to realize that his face looked so familiar to me. As the interview continued, somehow we got off-track, and we both discovered we had graduated from the same high school, in the same year. I remembered that he was voted most likely to succeed in high school. And I thought to myself. What are the chances of this happening? Andrew Jackson, the nerd from high school, now interviewing me for a job. It was at this time that I could hear God's voice himself. God said to me, "This job is yours." All I had to do was claim it. It was almost instantly, I felt a burden had just been lifted off of my shoulders. The rest of the interview went so well. Mr. Jackson had done everything except tell me I was hired, right there on the spot.

The next thing I had to do was take a basic math test, just to make sure that I could grasp the concept of the job. I passed the test with flying colors. I guess I wasn't that dumb after all. At the end of the interview, Mr. Jackson said that he had a few more interviews to do, and he would be making a decision on Monday morning. I said, Thank you, and I hope to hear from you soon." Once I got home, I emailed a follow-up letter to Mr. Jackson, thanking him for the interview opportunity.

Now the wait game begins. It seemed like Monday morning would never get here fast enough. Around 12:00P.M. on Monday, my cell phone rang. It was Mr. Jackson. He said "Stephanie, I want to offer you the accounting position." The starting pay is $45,875 per year. He told me I would start off with a two week vacation, six personal days, and tuition reimbursement." He then asked me if I had any questions for him. I said, No sir, I don't." Mr. Jackson then asked "Well ok, so would you like to accept the job?" My initial thoughts were *hell yeah*! But keeping it professional, of course I stated, "Yes, Mr. Jackson, I do accept the offer." Thank you so much for this opportunity!" I then asked him when he would like for me to start. He said, "Within a week, if possible. The person that would be training you will be transferring to another department within two weeks, and I want her to train you prior to her transferring." I told him that he could count on me, and I that would be there.

The very next thing I did was call my girl Daja to give her a status update. I was so excited when she answered the phone I began screaming at the top of my lungs. She said, "Girl, what's the matter with you?" I said, "Daja, I got the job!" It took a moment to sink in, and I repeated myself, "Daja, did you hear me? I got the job!"

She was so happy for me that she started screaming too! We were both so excited! Once we calmed down she said, "Stephanie girl, we gotta have a girl's night out! We have to celebrate the beginning of a new you, a happy you, and most importantly, an independent you!" Daja said, "We're going to party like it's 1989!" And when I say we brought the house down, thats exactly what we did!

Daja called some of our mutual friend, and we met up at this new spot in Atlanta by the name of Code Zero. It was my first time there, but some of the other girls had been there before, and it was at the top of the list for the night. As soon as I arrived at the club, I was really impressed with the complimentary valet parking, because there's nothing free when it comes to parking in the "A." And the club itself was real nice, and clean. I have to always check that out, whenever I plan to eat out. But everything was really on point. The men there were very respectful and not sloppy drunks telling lies. Even the DJ was great! She had all the latest songs. She even had some oldie's but goodie's too. We danced for what seemed like hours, had a few drinks, and met some really nice people. It was all good, and I can't wait until we do it again.

This is something that I should've done such a long time ago. I felt like a new woman. For the first time in a long time, my mind seemed to be free of all the mental chains, and burdens that I've allowed to hold me back. And I felt great!

My heart seemed to be a little lighter now. As I danced, and listened to the music, I began to feel my strength coming back. I had lost my sense of independence, and the sad thing is I didn't even realize it until this very moment. It's weird how your life can change right before your eyes. Sometimes, the changes are so subtle they're difficult to notice. And before you know it, your life feels like a roller coaster ride you desperately want to get off, but you just don't know how.

I made a promise to myself, and the Good Lord above, that this would be the last time I allowed someone to take me somewhere mentally that I didn't want to be emotionally. This was the first time, in a long time I was finally doing me! And you know something, it felt damn good, and I liked it!

By now, it was about 1:00A.M., so I told the girls that I was about to head out. I wanted to make sure that I got my praise on tomorrow, and Church started at 11:00A.M., and I didn't want to be late. So I was out! I gave everyone a hug, and thanked them so much for their support, and called it a night.

On my way out of the door, this guy by the name of Cashes approached me, and asked me if he could walk me to my car. Being that I didn't know this man, of course I said no thank you. I explained to him that my car was valet parked. He said ok that he understood that, but if he could have a little conversation with me while I waited for my car? I said, "Of course." He began to tell me that he noticed me dancing, and that I was such a beautiful young lady. He went on to ask me if I was married. I quickly told him no, that I was single, and loving every moment of it, and I thanked him for the compliment. He asked me if I come to this spot often, and I said, "No, this is my first time here, and I do plan to come again real soon."

By this time my car had arrived, and I had to leave. Cashes quickly asked if we could exchange numbers, I said, "Yes, that's fine." We exchanged numbers, and I got in my car, and pulled off.

It's Sunday morning, and of course I feel jacked up. I'm so tired, and I can barely keep my eyes opened. I have the worst hangover from drinking last night. But I said to myself, *the devil is a liar.* If I can make it to the club, then I'm gonna make it to church. When I finally arrived at church, the choir was singing so beautifully this particular Sunday. I mean, the choir always sounds great! But it was something special about this Sunday. It was as if the choir was singing directly to me. I'm not sure why this is. It could be pure coincidence, but that's my story, and I'm sticking to it. All I can say is the choir didn't sing this Sunday morning. They down-right sang this morning!

And when the Word came from Pastor Washington, I knew God was delivering me from everything that I'd been through. Pastor Washington preached on, "Letting Go of the Past." If you don't let go of the past it will eventually begin to affect your future. Pastor Washington also stated that in life we will all have some mountains, hills and valleys to climb. And we should expect that some of those mountains, hills and valleys will be bigger than others. He went on to say, it's not if you will come up against these obstacles that should be your concern, but being strong enough to overcome those obstacles when you do come up against them should be your focus. This is when you should reach for your armor, and call on the name of Jesus, and ask God to give you the strength to go around these mountains, climb over those hills and walk through those valleys. Because every obstacle in your life is not meant to be moved; some obstacles are strategically placed in your life to help you grow, and reach your full potential. But when your load becomes too heavy, and your strength is weak, that's when you should straight up ask God to carry you. He said, "We're taking it straight to the hood today. We're going to straight up talk to God. Pastor said "Now, I'm sure everyone knows about that secret closet, right?" He said, "If you don't know, you better ask somebody, because at some point in this life, we're all going to need it."

Pastor Washington went on to say, "If you want to become successful, then you have to speak success into your life, and don't accept anything less. There's power in the tongue, and you can speak life, and death into any situation. Failure is never an option! It's just an easy way out!

It was then, that I began to say, *Lord, I hear you! I hear you loud, and clear! Even though this church is full of people, I know this Word is for me, and it's not for anyone else but me.*

At that time I began to cry and claim my deliverance. I gave the Lord my promise that I would never look back! From this point on in my life, I'm moving forward!

This was the first time in a very long time, I felt like my season had finally come. And now, I truly understand the big picture; that in order to be a better mother to my children, I must first be a better person to myself, and stop allowing myself to be a victim, and holding onto anger, and things that I cannot change. Basically, at the end of the day, I have to let go and let God. And since I do pray, then I'm not gonna worry!

A LITTLE QUOTE TO LIVE BY:

"What's for you is only for you, and not anyone else!!! But you have to go, and get it, because even the milk man doesn't deliver to your door anymore!"

Chapter
10
Making Money

As I begin to get ready for work, I turned on the radio to listen to one of the hottest radio stations in Atlanta. All the DJ's are full of energy, and so funny! This is exactly what I needed to get my morning started. The kids were up, and getting ready for school now, and all I can do is, tell God *thank you.* I'm so blessed to be in a much better place now. God is really working with me on the inside, and I can see it showing on the outside. Today, everyone in the house, including me, has something to do this morning, and it feels great!

I had forgotten how liberating it feels to make your own money, and not depend on a man, or anyone else to take care of your each, and every want, and need.

It's so easy to become mentally trapped, and to lose your self-worth in a relationship, where the man makes all the money. Most women would love the opportunity to stay at home, and take care of the kids, while their man works and brings home the money. Back in the day, that's what a real man was supposed to do.

The problem with this type of relationship is that most women become *lost* and *powerless*. There's an old saying, that *the person that makes the money, makes all the rules*. Therefore, if the woman doesn't work, she's instantly put into an inferior position in the relationship, and that's a terrible place to be. In fact, it's a very lonely place to be. Trust what I say. It's not what I heard; it's what I know.

I would advise any woman to make sure that she always stands on her own two feet. Never allow a man, to hold all the cards in the relationship, because if you do, then you will always have to play his game. And most times you will not like the rules of the house. It's also very important to start your new relationship off the way you would want it to continue. It's difficult to break old habits. Men are like babies. When a child is born, it's pure and innocent and a whole lot of fun. It's the same with men, and a new relationship. Babies must be taught right from wrong, and so do men. If you give them an inch, they'll take a mile, and go against the grain. Trust me, they always do. You have to teach, and show your man how you want to be treated, right out the gate. You have to bend the sap while it's young; because the older it gets the tougher it gets. I didn't do that. And I've always regretted it!

It's like this, if you want your man to cook for you sometimes, I'm telling you, make sure, when you begin the relationship that he cooks for you sometimes. If you don't start your relationship out that way, it's going to be hell trying to get him to cook later. The same thing applies to cleaning, and grocery shopping. If you want your man to do these types of things for you later, then make sure, and start him off doing those type things. If you don't, you'll find yourself being a domestic partner, and you might as well put your apron on. And I mean that literally. It will always be expected that the woman in the relationship will always do all of the cooking, all of the cleaning, and all of the grocery shopping. So ladies take note. Always start things off the way you would like for them to continue. That's what I've finally learned. As for me and my future relationships, I'm not settling anymore! The last relationship I played by his rules. The next relationship, I'm holding all the cards, and he's playing by mine, and I plan on being trump-tight at all times.

Now that the kids are on the bus, I'm going to head out for work with my coffee in hand. And if I must say so myself, *I'm looking fabulous!* Once I arrived at work, I met Julie. She is the lady that will train me for my new position. She walked me through the office, introduced me to everyone, and told me what everyone's position was. After all that was over, it was now time for me to get to work. To my surprise, I understood everything that Julie was explaining to me up to this point, and everything was going very well.

My on-the-job training was supposed to last about two weeks. But since I understood the material so quickly, Julie sort of let me work alone before the end of the week. By Tuesday of the following week I was totally on my own, and if I must say so myself, I was *doin' the damn thang!*

Mr. Jackson checked on my progress many times during my first week. However, on Thursday of the second week, he told me to keep up the good work. He also made the comment that he knew he had made the right decision when he hired me. I said, thank you, and I was smiling from ear to ear.

Today is Friday. And on the first Friday of every month the company has a luncheon for all the new hires. The food was catered by a local Atlanta restaurant by the name of CozyFloyd's. This was the best Barbecue Ribs, Potato Salad, and Baked Beans I've tasted outside of my grandmother's. I don't know what they put in it, but the homemade barbecue sauce was out of this world. And don't get me started on the homemade Potato Salad, and sweet Baked Beans. I caught myself licking my fingers a couple of times. I was like *man this is so good!* I felt so greedy at the company luncheon too; I was even tired of seeing myself eat. I thought to myself, *this is a darn shame to be so greedy.* But everyone made me feel so at home, and a part of the family that it didn't really matter to them how much I ate or that I tried everything more than once.

Today was also my first pay day. They don't hold anything in the hole like most jobs do. And my check was fat! I thought to myself, *now, I can finally get on my feet, and get ahead. I can buy my kids some nice clothes, and still pay my bills without struggling so hard.* Also, I just began to get my child support check on a regular basis. This is going to be a big help to my kids and me, because they've really hung in there with their ma'ma. And they've never complained.

David always claims that he never has any money. Or should I say, he never has any money for me! Whenever I call him, and he does finally decide to answer his phone, he's always crying broke. Or, should I say, he's always crying broke to me. But whatever, because whenever I do see him, he's always dressed nice and lookin ' good. You can never catch him in something less than what's in style. I mean his shoes, look better than our son's and that's a damn shame.

The last time that I saw David, I told him that these children aren't just my responsibility. They're both of our responsibility. And if he doesn't get himself together and start giving me some money, then I'm going to put his ass on child support. I mean it! David has been gone for such a long time now, and he still hasn't given me one dime to help support our children. Now that's just plain sorry!

To be quite honest, at this point, David really doesn't care what I have to say. He thinks that I'm all bark and no bite. I guess he tried to call my bluff, and I answered his call. He just knew that I wouldn't put him on child support. But I had something for him, and I showed him a thing or two. I put him on child support! And I'm not taking him off either. It's really a shame how a man can just walk away from his responsibilities and automatically thinks he's single and fancy free! I just don't understand it! I guess the old saying *ma'ma's baby, daddy's maybe* is a true statement.

But it doesn't matter to me anymore, because David got just what he deserved. His ass is on paper now! And let him miss just one payment. I wish he would! Im'ma be on that phone like white-on-rice! It's like this! He had to get him, him. And now it's time for me to get, me, me!

When David left us, he could care less about how we were going to eat, and much less survive. And now, I don't give a damn about him being on child support. You know the saying, "It ain't much fun, when the rabbits got the gun." I guess now I'm the rabbit!"

This is something I've never been able to understand. Why does a complete stranger have to step in to make a sperm donor, not a father, provide support for his children? You can put this on everything I love: If David doesn't pay his child support, and I mean pay it on time, he will just end up in jail, the state will suspend his driver's license or I'll get that income tax check. It's whatever, because it's all green, and spends the same to me and I'll take it however it comes. But all I can say is; it better come!

It's time for him to grow up and get his shit together! I didn't have an option, so why should he? And I'm not changing my mind either. I just won't do it! I know him like the back of my hand. He wants everything to go his way or no way.

He's going to give it a few days for things to cool down, and then he'll call me and try to mess with my emotions. But I don't care what he says or how much he begs, and pleads for me to take him off child support, it's not happening! I didn't make these children by myself, and I'm not going to take care of them by myself.

Why should I? So he can have more money to spend on his other women. I don't think so. They all better like going to the burger joint, because that's the only place he's going to be able to afford to take them. At least they're going to make out better than me. He didn't even want to take me there. So I guess they should consider themselves lucky, especially, if he allows them to order a combo meal, with his cheap ass self. This is too funny. But it's better them than me.

I'm so glad that I'm in a better place now. It's been several months, and my job is still going great, and I like the people that I work with too. I've also been enrolled in college for two semesters now, and my grades are great. I was only a few credits short from getting my degree, so why not.

If I hadn't stopped going to college years ago when I first met David, I would've graduated with my bachelor's degree in accounting by now. But it's ok, better late than never. And since my company offers tuition reimbursement, there's no better time than now for me to take advantage of it, while I can.

A LITTLE QUOTE TO LIVE BY:

"You get out of life exactly what you put into it. If you put a little in, then you'll get a little out. Never stop dreaming, because your dreams are the footprints that will lead you directly towards your future."

Chapter
11
Girls Weekend Out

This weekend all my girlfriends and I have decided to have a girl's weekend out. We're not going to have any kids, husbands, or boyfriends with us. The plans are to meet up at the spa. Everyone is going to have a massage, facial, pedicure, and a little Wine. We're just going to kick back this weekend enjoy ourselves, and chill. It's going to be a drama free weekend, strictly for the ladies. After all the fluff-stuff, we're going to go out, have dinner and then end the night at the club. The plans are to meet-and-mingle just a little and dance a whole lot.

Now that I'm finished working out with DaShaun, it's time to take a shower. After I get dressed, I'll drop the kids off at my Uncle Eric's house for the weekend. I'm so blessed to have my uncle in my son's life. He spends a lot of time with him, and he's also a great role model too. I called and asked if the kids could come over for the weekend. He said, "Sure," that he would love to have the kids over, without any hesitation at all.

Now that everyone is ready, and the kids are in place, it's time to head out to the spa. I am so excited about this weekend. I feel it's very important for all women to get out, have some fun, and enjoy the essence of their femininity sometimes. It's important, and most women don't do it enough, and I was once one of those women. We spend so many of our best years caring, and loving everyone else that we forget to take some time out to love, and care for ourselves.

While all of the girls are relaxing and having a drink of wine, we all say at the same time "This is something we should've done a long time ago! This is so overdue!" I continued to say, "It's all good. It's better late, than never! And even though this might be our first, it surely won't be the last." We all did a toast to that statement. Now that everyone has had their spa treatment, we headed back to our hotel rooms, and prepared to get ready for dinner. We all decided to have some Japanese Hibachi food for tonight. Hibachi food is not just great to eat, but the way it's cooked is so entertaining. We went to the Hibachi restaurant located on Peachtree Street in downtown Atlanta, and the cook, Marlo, was so funny.

He did some really neat tricks when he was cooking. He tossed an egg behind his back, and cracked it with the spatula, before he cooked it. This was such a trip. If I had tried that, the whole egg would've landed on someone's head, or the floor, but never on the spatula. Every one of us was very pleased with their food choices for the night. We ate so much, but none of us could finish everything, so we packed up what we had remaining, and we were ready to head to the club, to dance off some of the calories we just consumed.

When I say everyone of us were some sexy ladies that night, I mean every last one of us was *handling our business.* And since this was such a special weekend for all of us, we rented a limousine for the night to take us around the city before we went to the club.

I've always known Atlanta was a beautiful city. However, I didn't realize how pretty Atlanta was at night, under the stars, and on this particular night the city seemed more beautiful than ever to me, and the skyline was just amazing. Every star seemed to have its own special meaning, and shined so brightly. As I gazed in amazement at the sky, I had to pinch myself to make sure I was still awake. I wanted to make sure all this was real, and I wasn't dreaming, and most of all, that this was happening to me. I can't put my finger on it, but there was something extra special in the air surrounding the city tonight, and I wish I could stay in this moment forever.

When we finally arrived at our destination, all my girls, including me, fell into the club. And when I say, we fell into the club, that's exactly what we did. If I must say so myself; we almost shut the club down when we walked in. Within the next ten minutes, all of us were on the dance floor, dancing. We were having so much fun. To my surprise, I didn't know that my guy-friend, Cashes was going to be in the club that night. Just like the last time, he spotted me from way across the room.

As soon as I finished dancing, and went over to the bar to buy myself a drink, he stepped to me and said, "Hello beautiful!" I tried to play it off, like I didn't hear him. He then repeated himself, "Hello, beautiful lady!" This time I turned around and said, "Hi there, how are you?" He responded that he was doing wonderful, now that he had spotted me. Cashes ordered me a drink, he sat down a little while, and we had great conversation. Then we went on the dance floor and had a great time. As we were dancing, I looked to my right and who did I see? It was David standing over there in the corner just staring me down. I was like *damn, if his eyes were guns, I would have been shot dead by now.*

After I noticed David, I really got my swag on then. It was so funny to see him standing over there looking jealous. But I didn't care—I just ignored his ass to the fullest. Then my slow jam came on, and why did that have to happen? Cashes, and I just continued to dance, and be in the moment, and while we were dancing, and moving to the music he went in to give me a kiss on the forehead. As the song progressed so did we. We began to grind to the beat of the music. I could feel him pulling me closer and closer to him as we continued to dance. If the truth be told, I really didn't care. I could tell we were both beginning to feel a romantic attraction coming on, and before I knew it, he kissed my nose, then he licked the front of my lips, and by the time the song was over, he went in for the full kiss. His lips were as soft as cotton. I couldn't help but give him back everything he was giving me. I can't lie. I tried playing hard to get, but I was so horny and lonely, I couldn't help but kiss him back. He made me feel so sensual and sexy. Something I haven't felt in years, and I haven't been with a man since David left.

During all this time, David just continued standing there, staring at us. As soon as Cashes stepped away for a few moments to go to the restroom, David had the nerve to step to me, and ask me if he could buy me a drink.

I looked at him, and politely said, "Really. You want to buy me a drink?"

David said "Yes, of course. Why wouldn't I?"

I just looked at him, and said nothing.

Well, may I?

I said, "No I'm fine."

Then he came with that tired-ass line. The line that's been used since my granddaddy's day, "I can see that!" I thought to myself, that's so from the sixties, and rolled my eyes at him.

Then he went on to say. "You sure look good tonight, and I see that you've lost a lot of weight too."

"I said really. I can't believe that you noticed? But thank you anyway." I was still treating him as-cold-as ice. I know he could feel those icebergs hanging off his ass. It was so funny to see him sweating. He went on to ask me how the kid's were doing. And I said to him, "If you pick up the phone, and call them sometimes, you might know how they're doing. But anyway, they're doing just fine."

Shortly, after this Cashes walked up to the table and I introduced him to David. They shook hands, dapped each other up, and then David walked away, looking like a sad puppy with that same stupid look on his face. You would have thought he had gotten slapped in the face with an ugly stick, the way that face was looking. I just turned away, smiled, and kept on doing my thing. In my mind, he was so last year. He may as well keep on moving, because I sure am.

By this time, it was around 2:00A.M., and everyone was ready to end the night. All the girls danced to one more song while we waited for the limo to pick us up, and take us back to the hotel. At this point, all of us were very tired. When we got back to the hotel room we tried to talk about how much fun we had this weekend, but before we knew it, we all fell asleep, just where we were sitting.

On Sunday, just before checking out of the hotel, my phone rang, and it was David. I asked him what was up, and he said that he wanted to see what plans I had later on in the day.

I told him that I was going to rest, because I had a long weekend. I was tired and I had to be to work on Monday at 8:00A.M., and I didn't want to be late. He said that he could understand that, but he wanted to know when he could take me out for dinner so that we could talk.

I told him that I wasn't sure, and I would get back in touch with him about it. I began to think to myself. You've got to be kidding me. All those years we were together, he never wanted to take me anywhere. He really has some nerve. And whether he knows it or not; he's not a priority on my list right now. I guess he didn't miss what he had until it was gone. He was always giving me one lame excuse after another as to why I couldn't go out with him. Now he wants to take me out to an expensive restaurant. I never would have thought in a million years that I would have this dilemma. Wow, all I can say is this:

he's to funny, but I'm really not interested. As of right now, I don't think I'm going to take him up on his offer, either.

I really don't want to go anywhere with David. My life is at happy place, and I don't want him anywhere in or around it, trying to mess things up for me. Oh yeah, I almost forgot unless I'm picking up my child support check. And baby, ain't nothing or nobody stopping that check!

A LITTLE QUOTE TO LIVE BY:

"Balance is an important ingredient for a successful and happy life. So remember, if you work hard; you have to play even harder! Always take time out for yourself, because no one will love and take care of you, better than you can."

Chapter
12
Moving Forward & Changing my Tomorrow's

I'm so grateful that I can finally see and appreciate my tomorrows. It's been a long time coming. I have a job that I love, and a place that I can finally call my own now. And as I look around, I can't believe it's almost been a year since David walked out on us. Since that time, I've re-enrolled back in college, and completed two semesters of school. The best thing about all of this is—if I continue to stay on track, I will graduate during the summer of next year. I will finally have my bachelor's degree in accounting, something that's long overdue. I'm so blessed. Well, like everyone always says, "Only the strong will survive." Most women are stronger than they give themselves credit for. I know this first hand, because I was once one of those women.

I'm so grateful, that I finally realized how blessed I truly am. At one point in my life I was so focused on all the things that I didn't have, that I completely lost sight of the things that I did have. I didn't have a clue how I was going to make it, and get back on my feet. But I guess God had a plan for me that I didn't know anything about. My life didn't begin to change until I decided to let go of David both mentally and physically. And I feel all changes have been for the better. It's the strangest thing. It's almost like David being in my life was blocking my blessings or something. I really don't know what else to say. It's something I can't even explain.

You see, as I think back a little; I thought that I was in love with this man. Whatever treatment he wanted to give me, I just accepted it, even though deep down in the bottom of my gut I knew something wasn't quite right. Nevertheless, when everything was all said and done, it wasn't David's fault at all. It was all mine. The truth is David couldn't do anymore to me than I allowed him to do. If you want to call him anything—then call him an opportunist. Everyone loves a great opportunity. I was his, and he seized the moment. That's all there is to it, nothing more, and nothing less.

Nevertheless, at the time I didn't realize it, but, if I'd loved myself half as much as I'd loved David, then my life would be in a much better place today. It's like my grandma always said, "Baby, you're never too old to learn." So I guess David was the teacher, and he took me back to school. Now the table has turned a little, and he's back in class.

Little did I know, David leaving me was the best gift he could've ever given me. If he hadn't decided to leave me, I'd probably still be in that tired, broken relationship. I guess the old saying that "God looks out for fools, and babies," really makes sense to me now.

But karma is real sweet, because for some strange reason, David's been calling me like crazy, ever since he saw me in the club. To be quite honest—I haven't made any time for him. Almost every time he calls, I never answer the phone. Instead, I let his call go straight to my voicemail. There's no need for him to ask me anything at all about taking him off child support, because it's not going to happen. As far as I'm concerned, David and I really don't have anything to talk about, unless it involves the kids. But I know he's up to something. I just can't put my finger on it.

In his last voice message, David said that he wanted to take me out to eat at this nice restaurant located in Buckhead. I guess he's trying to *flex* or something. Perpetrating like he's on baller status now. You see, Buckhead is this really nice area located in downtown Atlanta. The restaurants located down there aren't cheap either. I really hope he's not trying to impress me, because it's not working. Frankly, I could really care less.

I must admit. I have been giving it a lot of thought, but I still haven't made a firm decision yet, or returned his call, to give him an answer. He can sweat a little. It won't hurt him a bit. His ass didn't care when I was calling him in the past, so what was good for me back then, is good for him now. He really gets on my last nerve, because he knows me so well. Really everyone knows that I have a weakness for good food, especially, when the bill's not on me.

However, the longer I sit here, and contemplate the idea; I'm seriously leaning more towards taking him up on his offer, than not. The truth is being angry is not a very good feeling, and if it lingers too long, it can fester, and leave blisters that may become permanent scars deep into your soul. At this point in my life, I've come to realize that anger is really a wasted emotion that only kills the person that's harboring it. And right now that person is me. I guess it won't hurt me to be nice, and kill him with kindness. This way he'll never find the murder weapon, and he might just think everything's all good between him and me. When the fact is, I'm mad as hell!

Well, since I've decided to take David up on his offer to take me out to dinner on Saturday night, I have to make sure that I'm looking my *absolute best*. I've lost about fifty pounds since he's left, and if I must say so myself; *I feel good and I look even better*. It's about time for David to come to grips with what he's passed up on. I guess he's finally realized. When one man won't, another man will. That's just keeping it real.

It's about 8:00P.M. on Saturday, and I am waiting to have my car valet parked. As I entered the restaurant, I noticed David was already sitting at the table waiting on me. I thought to myself, *ain't this a switch, and I like the direction this night is heading in already. For once he's waiting on me; just like he should be.*

Once I sat down, the first thing David does is tell me how beautiful he thought that I looked tonight. He continues to say how much he's really missed me these past months. As he continued to speak, I just gave him this look. You know the look, the *shut the hell up look.* I was so cold to him at first. It was like I had a hundred places I'd rather be, and being there with him was not one of them. I'm sure he could feel the chill, because I know that I did. After dinner was served, we continued to speak, and talk about the kids for a little while longer, and how they were doing in school. He just continued to make small talk, and I mean it was real small. If I didn't know any better, I would've thought that we were set up on a blind date, and only one of us liked our date. And that person wasn't me!

Once we placed our order for dessert, I finally asked David, "So David, why are we really here? Dinner will be over soon, so let's just skip all the small talk, and get straight to the point. Why did you really invite me out for dinner tonight?"

"Stephanie, I wanted to let you know that I really miss you. And I know that I made a big mistake leaving you, and the kids like I did. The old saying, *"you don't miss your water until your well runs dry,"* is a true statement. Let's just say, I've experienced that one for myself. And I'm thirsty as hell right now! I miss you and the kids much more than I ever expected that I would. And I really want to know if we could make small steps toward rebuilding our relationship?"

What I truly wanted to say was *Hell to the No!* But I didn't, I just allowed him to continue to talk, and make a complete fool of himself. Finally, after I was so tired of hearing his lies, I cut into his conversation. If I had not interrupted him, he would probably still be there, sounding pitiful.

I looked David straight into his eyes as I began to speak to him. I told him, "David, you know that I will always love you, right? I would be lying if I said anything different. I mean, we did spend many years of our lives together. But I'm no longer in love with you. Let's first be perfectly clear on that. Please understand you leaving me was a turning point in my life. It was truly a blessing in disguise. At times, I sit back and think about how I begged and pleaded with you just so you would stay with me, so we could work on what I thought was a relationship. I was so sure that I could make you love me; or at least I thought that I could. Regardless of how much I begged, and pleaded with you, all my efforts were in vain, because you left me anyway. The sad thing is, you didn't only leave me, but you left our children too."

"I'll man up, Stephanie. I know what I did was wrong. I should've given it more thought before I walked out, and left you, and my children the way that I did. It was really selfish of me. If I could, I would give anything to take it back, just so I could erase that day—trust me, I would. But I can't. All I can do now is say, I'm sorry, I truly, truly am."

"Yes David, I'm sure you are sorry now. And I don't know what I was thinking when I kept pleading with you to stay with me. I always knew love was blind, but I didn't know it could be stupid too. I thought us having children together would mean a little more to you than it did. And whether I wanted to admit it or not, I had to grow up and understand that a baby doesn't keep a man. It never has, and obviously, it never, ever will. I have the T-shirt on that deal. But David, you know the biggest lesson I've learned from being with you?"

"What's that, Stephanie?"

"I've learned that a woman should never, ever have to beg her man for affection, and to spend time with her. If it's true love, it has to be free of any coercion. A man has to love his woman, and be with his woman, just because he wants to, nothing more, and nothing less. It's as simple as that. If I had accepted your actions for what they really were; you wouldn't have had to leave me. I would have left you years ago!"

"Stephanie…"

"Please let me finish! I've been holding onto this hurt and pain inside my heart for a really long time. I need this opportunity to finally get it out of my system, without any interruptions."

"You're right. I do owe you that much."

"Thanks, now back to what I was saying. I really want to apologize. Not just to you, but to the lady you brought to my uncle's house."

"Stephanie, I don't think that's necessary."

David notices the waiter, and waves for him. He's nervous about the direction this conversation is heading.

Excuse me. May I have the check please?

The waiter replies yes, and leaves to retrieve the check.

"Sorry about that, you can continue."

"As I was saying—this is something I have to do for me, not you. I want to be free mentally. I want you to understand the main reason that I beat her up wasn't because she was with you. It was because she was being rude, and not respecting me, and my house. She wasn't acting like a lady-so I didn't treat her like one."

"Ok, you're right."

"I must admit. I did handle that situation very immaturely with ole girl, but she really pissed me off! She was really being a jerk. However, if I think about it, at the end of the day, she really didn't owe me anything. However, if you were to ask me could she have been more respectful? My response would be, 'Yes,' because a real lady should always know her boundaries, especially when it comes to dealing with a man, and the mother of his children. That's a very touchy area, and when you cross certain lines, things can get real messy. However, I do feel the next time she's told to calm it down; she'll back the hell up, and stay in her lane. Crossing the solid line into someone else's lane could be hazardous to your health."

David just stares, and smirks at this statement.

"However, once I cooled down and really gave it some thought. I had to ask myself, why the hell should I expect for another woman to respect me, when you don't even respect me? I mean really, if you think about it, I don't mean a single thing to her; she could care less about me. But who I should've meant something to was you! So if the truth be told, instead of whipping up on her, I really should've been whipping up on your ass! So my apologies this one's on me."

The waiter shows up with the check, and David's glad for a brief break in the conversation.

"It's ok. I understand why you reacted the way that you did. And I have to agree, I was totally out of line for disrespecting you, and my kids by bringing her over there. So please accept my apology. It will never happen again. I can promise you that much."

"Thanks David. Now I know I've been speaking for quite a while, but trust me, I'm almost done. But before I finish, I just want to say thank you."

"Why are you thanking me?"

"No, really thanks. I just want to thank you for leaving me."

"Excuse me."

"Yes, if you hadn't left me; more than likely, I would still be that little seed under the dirt. But God recognized something I was too weak to see. He recognized that it was time for me to blossom. And since I wasn't strong enough to move you on my own, God moved you for me. So again, thank you. Thank you for all the hurt, and all the pain that I've been through, just for loving you. Because in my quest of loving you; I found me."

"Oh yeah, one last thing. You know in our past, we've had our share of arguments, right?"

"Yeah, of course, I do."

"You know normally, I would just sit, and listen to everything you had to say—whether or not, I agreed or disagreed with you. But there's one particular thing that you said to me when we had our last big argument that I will never forget. You said to me, 'It wasn't me. "It was you!' You know what, the more I thought about it; the more I begin to realize that wasn't true at all. It was never you! It has always been me! I gave you too much power in our relationship. More importantly, I gave you too much power over me! Please believe, this will never happen to me again, not by you, or anyone else. It's ok, because *fool me once, shame on you. Fool me twice, makes me the damn fool!* And I'm not willing to be anyone's fool ever again! To be quite honest with you, the Stephanie you see sitting here now isn't the same Stephanie that you walked out on. I'm much stronger and much wiser now. And if I didn't learn anything else from being with you, what I did learn was that my focus was in the wrong place. I spent all those years—all my younger years, trying to change you, when the truth is, I should've been working on changing me."

"Stephanie, I'm sorry you feel the way that you do. My intentions were never to disappoint, and hurt you so much. Will you ever be able to forgive me?"

"David, you've already been forgiven. In order for me to heal, reach my full potential, and become the very best woman that I know I can be—I have to forgive you, and let you go. There's absolutely no other choice for me!"

"I still love you Stephanie!"

The waiter comes back to the table to collect payment for dinner. And he was told to return in fifteen minutes.

"Do you really love me David, or are you in love with my *Potential*, and what I can do for you?"

David just frowns, and he doesn't say a word.

"Now with all that said, I would like to thank you for a lovely evening and a fantastic dinner. This has meant more to me than you'll ever know. However, I must say that I've moved on now, and I suggest that you do the same. But to answer your question, no, it's over! We're over! There will never, ever be another you and me again. I refuse to look back. At this point in my life, I'm only looking forward. That's just how it is!"

"Stephanie, please don't leave! I know that you've made some major advances in your life since I left, and I'm very happy for you. But you can't deny the fact that you still love me. Let's just be honest with one another. You know there's no other man that can make you feel as good as Big Daddy can! You know that right? Have you forgotten that I can read your body language? And I can see deep into your soul through your eyes."

"Wait, wait let me get this straight! Did you just say Big Daddy?"

David moves his chair closer to Stephanie. And he begins to whispers in her ear.

"Yes, don't you miss it? I know you remember back in the day when things were all good between us. How I would lay you down on your stomach, then I would proceed to caress, and kiss each and every inch of your body from top to bottom. Then I would flip you over onto your back, and spread your legs from side to side, remember back then? That's when you liked it a little ruff. Next, I would slowly kiss, and lick every inch of your body until I reached your toes, and then I would suck each, and every one of them, one at a time—just before I would sink myself deep down into you. And baby once I got in—you know you were all mine. I know it's been some time ago—but I know you haven't forgotten about those good old days. Back then we were so open, and free with each other. I really miss those times, and I would like for us to make new memories just like those or even better. Like I said before Stephanie, I still love you.

Regardless of what anyone else may think, I know that the two of us standing together have always been much stronger than just one of us standing alone."

Stephanie moves back from David.

"Please shut up! This is exactly what I'm talking about. The first thing you need to do is check out getalife.com. This is one of my biggest problems with most men. They think sex will make everything all better, and the hell with communication and affection. It's obviously you didn't get the memo. This is so far from the truth. All I want to know is where the hell are the flowers, the candy, or the simple I'm a jackass card? Men never want to deal with the real issues at hand, and you're no different. I guess now that you've had a little time to graze a few more fields, and play around a little bit, I'm supposed to take you back, and be alright with everything you've done to me in the past. You better recognize, because that's not how things are going down, right here! Not to mention, I feel like you're so full of shit!"

"Why do I have to be all that?"

"To be honest, you're really all that and some! I don't think you fully understand what you just said to me? Do you have a clue what I've gone through this past year? Because I don't think you do! So let me break it down for you real quick."

"I didn't want to go there with you, but I think I better. First of all, the way you handled the money in the bank was totally out of order. The first thing you did was run your ass down to the bank, and take out all the money from the accounts. You didn't even leave me $7.00 total between both accounts. Now you're probably broke, and you think I'm supposed to forget that ever happened? How could you do this to me? Explain this please!"

"Stephanie, all I can say is I was being selfish. I was only thinking about myself at that time, and I apologize for that. I'm truly sorry. I truly am!"

"Yeah, you're right! At least we agree on one thing. You are sorry!

The next thing that happened was my embarrassing eviction! Because of you, everything that I owned in this world was put out on the street. I was evicted from my home, David! Do you have any idea how that feels? Oh yeah, of course you don't! You left! I had to deal with this situation all alone with two kids! I had to explain to them why we were put out on the street-not you! There were many days that I had no money, with two kids to feed! There were even times we had no food in the refrigerator to eat, and this is just a small picture of the hell that I've been through, after you left. And after all of this you have the nerve to step to me with some Big Daddy shit! Answer this for me. Who the hell do you think you are? I wouldn't want to be with your trifling ass if you were the last man standing here on earth! All I can say is you really need to stop it! You sound like such a hypocrite to me right now. Not to mention that I totally disagree with everything you just said. But there's one thing I know and two for sure—if I don't leave this restaurant right now—I'm going to lose the little bit of religion that I do have!"

"Stephanie, please don't walk away from me. Will you please stop and listen to me for just a moment?"

"Tell me, why should I listen to you David? All you've ever done was told me lies! No, I don't want to sit here, and listen to anything else you have to say! You've said quite enough already! There's really nothing left for us to talk about at this point! I'm sorry—but I'm done with this conversation, and I'm done with you! I hope you have a good life, but I will not be part of your little equation anymore!"

"So is this really what you want?"

"What the hell do you mean? Is this what I really want? Did you not hear anything I just said? Of course this is what I want! You were the one that said our destinations were not the same anymore—that we were on different paths now; and at that time, when everything was going your way; all your sorry ass could do is hope that I would understand, right?"

"Well, your wish has come true. I finally got it! And guess what—I don't want to be with you anymore! Truthfully, I never want to be with another man like you! I can't speak for you. However, as for me and my life— my *Mind, Heart, Body,* and *Soul* are in total sync right now. And I will not allow you or any other man to change my direction or the way that I feel! I can honestly say that I've finally learned the art of loving me just for me, with all my flaws and imperfections. And I love and appreciate each and every one of them—because each flaw and imperfection that I have is what makes me special in my eyes. It makes me Stephanie!"

"I'm getting up and leaving now, because I've had enough of all this nonsense! And I've had enough of you!"

The waiter returns with all this going on hoping to finally collect payment. Stephanie anxiously takes the check and pays the bill.

"Oh yeah, I forgot to mention it. Don't sweat the check tonight. This one's on me!"

David reaches out and grabs Stephanie's arm as she turns to walk away.

"Stephanie, what about the kids? We owe it to them to try and work things out!"

"David, you're welcome to come and spend time with your children. You just can't come and spend time with me. That's all there is to it!"

Stephanie snatches her hand away and walks toward the door.

"Stephanie, I'll call you tomorrow."

"Don't waste your time doing that. I'll be preparing for my trip to Italy tomorrow. Me and the girls will be leaving next Friday and I have a million and one things to do before I go. So my spare time will be very limited for the next couple of weeks. Good-bye David!"

Sentiments for the Soul:

In order to move forward in your life you must be able to face and accept the mistakes that you've made along the way. But what's most important is not just realizing the mistakes you've made, but not making the same mistakes over and over again.

In order for a change to be permanent a change must happen on the inside, because anything else is strictly on the surface and it won't last.

When you can no longer recognize the man you once loved. Love yourself more and let him go.

It's a complete waste of time trying to raise a grown man, put that time into yourself—because the time you spend trying to figure things out—God's already worked them out!